TWICE UPON A TIME

Robin Hood

The One Who Looked Good in Green

Don't miss any of these spellbinding stories from
Wendy Mass!

The Willow Falls series

11 Birthdays
Finally
13 Gifts
The Last Present
Graceful

The Twice Upon a Time series

Rapunzel: The One with All the Hair
Sleeping Beauty: The One Who Took the Really Long Nap
Beauty and the Beast: The Only One Who Didn't Run Away

TWICE UPON A TIME

Robin Hood

The One Who Looked Good in Green

WENDY MASS

SCHOLASTIC INC.

ISBN 978-1-338-34004-4

12 11 10 9 8 7 6 5 4 3 2 1 18 19 20 21 22 23

Printed in the U.S.A. 40

Originally published in hardcover by Scholastic Press, June 2018

This edition first printing, November 2018

Book design by Yaffa Jaskoll

For Chloe Brawer, my little mind reader.
You make every story better.

And with gratitude for editor extraordinaire
David Levithan, wearer of many hats, master of them all.
Thank you for slipping me a note fifteen years ago and
adding so much magic to my life.

Introduction

If you don't know much about the legend of Robin Hood and the lovely Maid Marian, you might say, "That's the one about the guy with the green tights and pointy hat who stole from the rich and gave to the poor, right?"

And you'd be correct. But this kindhearted thief, this brave and clever master of disguise, did not start out that way. Far from it, in fact. The young, carefree Robin was more likely to be getting in trouble than righting the world's wrongs or thinking of anyone but himself. At least, not until he met Marian, who never thought of herself at all. But in her defense, she didn't have much time to think, what with all the shopping.

Or at least, that's the story I'm going with. The original English folktales about Robin Hood are short on details about Marian (and don't have much more to say about Robin himself), so the version you're about to read is simply my best educated guess as to how it all went down. Plus, I've taken the liberty of combining the characters of Will Stutely and Will Scarlet. Because honestly, why are there two people named Will in the same folktale?

Also, it must be said, much of this takes place on another planet.

Before you dive in, though, if you're really attached to the old image of a swashbuckling Robin Hood and his band of Merry Men forced to flee to Sherwood Forest by the evil Sheriff of Nottingham and the cruel Prince John, allow me to direct you to Hollywood's collection of film adaptations. The characters even burst into song in some of them.

But if you're willing to go along for the ride with me, then sit back and enjoy this tale of two worlds — the first with glittering skyscrapers, orbiting spaceports, and food that wobbles when you try to eat it. The other is home to medieval outlaws, fearsome beasts who lick your feet, thick mossy woods, and dancing monks who can teach you the secret to everlasting life. For a price, of course.

And don't forget the spaceships. Only here they're called *airships* . . . and the next one is about to leave.

Try not to miss it.

CHAPTER ONE

↢ Robin ↣

Spaceport Delta Z, AD 2336

Swoosh! I lift my foot off the ground and my hoverboard glides exactly three inches above the rusty steel beams of Spaceport Delta Z. I'm not supposed to ride it outside of the Central Plaza, but I'm late for school and I never crash. Plus, I'm the kinda guy who believes you should ask for forgiveness instead of permission.

Ah, who am I kidding? I don't usually ask for forgiveness, either. But that's partly because my teacher is a robot, and I think it's bizarre to ask for forgiveness from a robot. And it's not like this is the kind of robot that looks like a person. We're talking square viewscreen for a head, one wheel for legs, and a body composed of leftover parts from a washing machine. We used to have real teachers up here, but none of them lasted more than a few months before they bought a one-way ticket on the next airship off this place. I don't blame them, really. Life on an old, remote spaceport like ours is not for the faint of heart.

I've heard many spaceports have bowling alleys and grassy fields, fancy restaurants serving fresh food, ice rinks, artificial gravity generators, luxury living quarters, and shops where you can buy every new gizmo and gadget in the galaxy. They even boast man-made lakes where you can take out a rowboat and toast the good life with a multicolored drink as you watch the airships lift off toward galaxies far, far away.

Spaceport Delta Z doesn't have any of that. Well, we have a gravity generator, but since it's my absentminded uncle's job to keep it running, we're guaranteed to be bouncing on the ceiling at least once a month. Otherwise, we're pretty bare-bones here. No cool shops, no luxury anything, and I've only tasted real food fourteen times in my life — once a year on my birthday.

Not that I'm complaining — not much, anyway. Our bodies can't even process real food more often than that. This is proven by the fact that after a birthday, no one wants to stand near you for a full two days until the food — always beans, onions, and corn — is out of your system and the air around you is safe to breathe again without retching.

Also, we have excellent music playing at all times in the plaza. There's no crime or vandalism, and very little fighting. Everyone's living space is exactly the same, and we're all given the same basic supplies and clothing, so there's no envy or greed. (Well, there may be *some* envy over my devilishly handsome face, but I can't help that!)

We do have one special activity — an arcade of video games that the station commander has built up over the years. Each kid is given an allotment of tokens each week that usually run out by the second day. My favorite game is a virtual reality game called BullsEye, where you shoot a virtual arrow at the screen and try to hit the center of these constantly moving circles. The only person who can come close to beating my high score is my cousin, Will, and he's thousands of points behind me.

Out of the forty-three full-time residents of Delta Z (although that number changes monthly as workers rotate in and out), Will is my only real friend (and he pretty much *has* to hang out with me due to us being related), but that's okay. As Uncle Kent says, I'm an "acquired taste." Not everyone gets me.

All things considered, this is a pretty good life. Better than being stuck on Earth, the only habitable planet in this solar system. Even though we're half a light-year away in the Oort Cloud, just thinking about that place makes me shudder.

"Catch!"

I expertly jump up and land backward on my board without missing a beat. The board slows and hums as it hovers outside Shane's Service Station and Garage. I reach out with one hand just as Shane — Delta Z's head mechanic — launches a round object at my head. I catch it right before it smacks me in the forehead.

"Nice," he says, and saunters back into his shop. Shane's a man of few words, but besides Will and Uncle Kent, he's the only other person I hang out with on a regular basis, and one of the only other "lifers" who never leaves this place. I open my palm to find a brand-new roll of clear tape. He must have won it in a poker game with a visiting pilot. That's how he gets most things.

"Yes!" I shout. "Thanks, Shane!" He gives me a wave as he disappears under a short-range shuttlecraft that he's been working on for two weeks. It's been decommissioned due to it tending to fall apart in outer space, but if anyone can get it up and running again, it's Shane. Just so long as no one tries to rush him. Then he'll toss his tools aside and play a few hands of the card game that runs all hours in the back of his garage until he's good and ready to work again.

I stick the tape in my pocket and zoom off again on the board, my mind racing with all the ways I can use this rare and precious item in my magic act.

Yes, I have a magic act. I can also ride a unicycle, juggle fire sticks, fence, and play speed chess — sometimes all at once. Hobbies are encouraged on Delta Z. Keeping us busy keeps us out of trouble. Or that's the idea, anyway. Cousin Will can speak four languages, jump five feet straight up, and bend his fingers completely backward until they're lying flat on the back of his hand. It's gross. But he's a big hit at parties.

I take a shortcut and turn down the narrow corridor that runs past the cargo bay where the storage rooms are located. Since we're primarily a transfer port between the planets in the three known star systems, none of the boxes or crates that arrive stay here long, a few days at most. One ship drops them off, and another picks them up. The cargo bay is off-limits to kids, which of course means I have to check it out whenever I'm in the area.

Today the room is bustling with activity, which is unusual. I pull up short and hop off my board, flipping it up and catching it neatly under one arm. I watch through the long window as workers in the same green outfit as I'm wearing wheel in solid black boxes of all different sizes, each marked *FRAGILE, DO NOT TURN UPSIDE DOWN*.

Half of them are upside-down.

The workers are stacking the boxes against the far wall, which means Delta Z is their final destination. I wonder what could be inside. Our monthly supplies already came last week, and these boxes are fancier than usual, made of some kind of composite material I haven't seen before.

I sniff the air. Food isn't supposed to travel between planets — something about microorganisms native to each individual planet being very dangerous somewhere else. If a tomato seed grown on one planet were planted in the soil of another, the damage could destroy the entire ecosystem of that planet. Our paltry birthday beans are sanitized for days before they're served. Still, every once in a while someone tries to sneak something off-world and it passes through here. We don't have any soil to risk contaminating, so storing contraband here isn't unheard of. But these boxes have no discernible smell, at least not from out here.

Under the *FRAGILE* warning I spot a row of smaller letters. I press my face as close to the window as I dare without smacking it with my forehead and drawing unwanted attention. Usually I'm a leap-before-I-look kinda guy, but Vinnie, the cargo delivery foreman, is a big dude who takes his job very seriously. Last time he found me hanging around here he chased me away with a vacuum cleaner. If I squint I can just make out the words:

PRIVATE PROPERTY OF LOCKSLEY MANOR

Huh. Weird. There's no one here named Locksley Manor. Or, wait . . . I think a manor might be another word for a fancy house. Either that or it's a six-legged biting toad that once thrived on planets with high levels of nitrogen in their atmosphere. I really should pay more attention when Roboteach talks.

As I stare at the words on the box, a vague, fuzzy scene

flits through my mind: a room made of glass walls, with something blue and white on the other side. I can't make out any details, though. This vision is followed by a whiff of something sweet, an odor I'm sure I've never smelled before. Then, as fast as it came, the scene is gone. It couldn't have been a memory. I've never been off Delta Z, and we don't have any place that looks or smells like that here.

I shake my head to clear it. The name *Locksley* must have conjured up something I read about in school, that's all. I move farther down the window toward the docking bay, hoping to spot the ship that made the delivery. Usually the pilot and any crew members will come aboard for a little break to stretch their legs, chat with us natives, maybe stop at Shane's to repair a part or play a hand of poker. Or at the very least they stay to refuel. But unless he did all that before unloading — which would be unusual — whoever delivered these boxes must have been in a big hurry because the docking bay is empty already. The arms that grab the arriving ships hang open, ready to pull in the next one.

I've spent much longer here than I should have. If I'm late for school again I'll have to "volunteer" at the waste disposal station all the way in the bowels (pun intended) of the spaceport.

The cargo bay workers have moved on to the next room, so the coast is clear. We get so little privacy on a spaceport this small, we need to take advantage of it when it comes our way. I'll just have to be quick.

I slip inside and scurry over to the closest stack. The boxes are all sealed up tight, with keypads on them that give no indication of the combination to spring open the lock. Maybe their weight will give a clue of their contents. I pick up the closest box. It's neither heavy nor light. I start to feel silly. They're probably something boring like spare parts for one of the oxygen machines that pump our air. I'll find out soon enough, anyway. Secrets don't stay that way for long here.

I replace the box in the pile and wind up jostling the one next to it. When it moves, I catch a glimpse of something red stuck between that box and the one behind it. I stare at the object. Red's not a color we ever see unless someone is bleeding. Color in general is rare. The nearby planets have all used up their natural resources, so there's basically nothing to make dyes out of, no clay, minerals, gems, berries, plants, flowers, or insects. The only reason our uniforms are green is because there's so much nickel alloy in the pipes here that our no-color clothes come out green after only one washing.

My hand reaches out of its own accord. I grab the tip of the strange object and pull, sliding out a long, soft, nearly weightless thing with a stiff yet flexible piece running down the center. My brain searches for the right word and I gasp a little when I register what I'm holding.

It's a feather! *A real feather!* I glide my hand down it, relishing the feel as the fluffy part slides between my fingers. I half expect the color to wipe off, but it doesn't. This feather was once a part of a living bird, and this was the *actual* color. No dye made this.

I've never seen an animal or a bird in real life. No one I know has. They're pretty much the stuff of legends, extinct for two hundred years on every planet known to humankind. And yet here is a feather.

I quickly run around the piles, peering between the boxes, but nothing else turns up. Since the boxes are all sealed, it must have gotten into the transport ship somehow, and then was gathered up with the delivery. How the workers missed it is anyone's guess. But I'm sure glad they did.

"Robin!" an annoyed voice growls from behind me. "What's your excuse this time? Got lost on the way to the schoolroom again?"

I move the feather behind my board and turn around to find the red-faced foreman. "Um, look, a ship's coming!"

He turns toward the empty expanse of space, and I run out before he can fetch his vacuum.

As soon as I'm clear of the cargo bay, I stash the feather in my pocket, hop on my board, and aim for the classroom doorway at the end of the long corridor. I've almost reached it when Will turns the corner and is suddenly right in front of me. I can't stop in time, so we bonk right into each other and topple backward. Actually, I probably could have stopped in time, but it's just more fun to knock each other over. This tells you how exciting my life usually is.

Will groans dramatically. "Robin! I think this time you've ruptured my spleen! I may only have moments to live!"

We both burst out laughing. That never gets old. Neither of us actually know what a spleen is, or what rupturing it would mean, but it's a line from an old video one of our teachers showed us a few years ago about when people used to get injured and their cells wouldn't automatically repair themselves after one injection from the nurse's medi-gun.

Robo-teach's head appears in the doorway. "Do you boys need a formal invitation to join the rest of your classmates?" For a robot, our teacher has a sarcastic streak that I have to admit I admire.

"We're sorry," Will says. He has no problem apologizing to people, including those made of metal circuitry and spare parts.

I follow Will into class and we join the others. The current population of kids on Delta Z is exactly nine. Our ages span from five (little Lisbeth) to sixteen (a rather fidgety boy named Toby who sings in his sleep — I know this because his family's home unit is next to ours). The best kid to cheat off of on a test is twelve-year-old Elan, whose hobby is memorizing the digits of pi, and the easiest kid to fool with a magic trick is ten-year-old Gabriella. I've gotten many extra tokens off of her as payment for my performances.

Such a large age spread means we spend our days doing anything from calculus to singing the alphabet. Today's lesson is about history, my least favorite topic. Up here most of us don't *have* a history. Why think about all that other people have lost?

As Robo-teach drones on about how something called *oranges* used to grow on something called *trees*, I slouch down low in my chair and pull out the feather. What kind of creature could it have come from? I twist it this way and that, noticing how the individual hairs clump together, then separate at the slightest touch. Would the creature have lived in a cold climate or hot? I've never felt extreme temperatures either way, so I can only wonder at the difference. Did it walk? Could it talk? *Do* animals talk? Maybe I should have tuned in a little more to the lessons after all.

I'm so absorbed in my find that it takes me much longer than it should to notice that Robo-teach and eight wide-eyed classmates have made a ring around my desk. Darn my remarkable ability to focus.

Robo-teach extends the pincher hook that is his hand, and after a brief hesitation, I place the feather in it. He drops the feather into a nook in his chest cavity, and soon images begin to flash in quick succession on his viewscreen of a face. Will and I exchange a look of surprise. What kind of new party trick is this? Has he always been able to do this?

"I am able to use the DNA of objects to trace their history," Robo-teach says, answering my unasked question. "It's a new program I'm experimenting with."

My brain has a hard time assigning words to the images I'm seeing in the pictures. A house, I think. An ocean. An egg? Or is that what they called an umbrella? Beasts with four legs, two legs, eight legs, wings! The images begin to slow, and then stop at a photo of a bird with shockingly bright blue, yellow, and red feathers. The letters below it spell out *MACAW*. This must be where my feather came from! Not this specific bird, of course, but one of that type. I could look at this macaw creature all day, but Robo-teach's screen has one last image to pull up, and this one is even odder.

A man with light brown hair, a square jaw, and bright green eyes is leaning against what looks like a real tree. Trees haven't existed for ages on the planet below us, or on any planets in the known star systems. The man — wearing a pointy brown hat — is holding a red feather with one hand and a piece of stiff fabric with his other.

"Long before digi-pens were invented, people used to dip the ends of feathers — called the quill — into ink to write with," Robo-teach explains. No one is paying attention. He continues anyway. "They originally made the ink from eggs, ash, and honey." When we continue to stare mutely at the screen, he adds, "Honey is a sticky material that is secreted from bees. Bees were flying, stinging creatures that —"

"Okay, okay, we get it," Toby interrupts. "Can the history lesson wait?"

We're not interested in the feather, the ink, the honey, the bees, or the fabric that Robo-teach will no doubt get to. We're looking at the man and the tree, and at the glowing yellow ball visible behind him, the one that's spilling light across the image. But we're mostly looking at the man.

Little Lisbeth gasps and throws her arms around my neck. "Robin! How did you get in that holo-picture?"

My mouth has gone dry. The man really *does* look like me. Or I look like him. Or what I'll look like in twenty years, anyway. I didn't time-travel into the past, age twenty years, and then pose for that picture, right? Or could I be related to this man somehow? I know nothing about my parents, or if I even have parents at all. Uncle Kent never speaks of how I came to live with him and Will, and I never question him. He and Will are all the family I need.

Lisbeth begins to cry, so I pull her on my lap and assure her, "It's not me, Lissy. Don't worry. I'm much more handsome than that dude, right?"

She sniffles, then smiles and nods. Will rolls his eyes, but I can tell by the straight line his lips have become that he's a little worried, too.

"Hmm," Robo-teach says. "A sample of your own DNA must have gotten on the feather and was picked up by my sensors."

This has our attention.

"DNA is a unique code in your body's cells," he explains. "This is how our nurse knows exactly how to cure you when you're hurt. If your DNA pulled up this image, this man is either you — which is impossible — or a long-ago relative along your father's line."

Now all the kids start talking at once, holding up their

fingers or a strand of hair, asking him to take a sample of their DNA, too.

"Our lesson is done for the day," Robo-teach says, shutting down the program and handing me back my feather. "Time for lunch."

I stash the feather in my pocket and grab my hoverboard from where it had been leaning against the wall. Time travel isn't real, so I know that wasn't me in that picture. There's got to be another explanation for our uncanny resemblance. I just don't know what it is.

Another way I know that wasn't me?

I've never seen the sun.

CHAPTER TWO

Marian

Earth, AD 2336

I have never seen the stars.

If I was ever going to spot them, it would be now, in the dark of night, when my toes are frantically gripping onto this slippery marble ledge, eighty-two stories above the grandest (and only) city left on Earth.

But no. Even up here the blinding lights shining from the one hundred skyscrapers that make up The City wash out any sign of the heavens. Add in the glowing lights of the airships' launchpads and the headlights of the hovercars, and I can almost fool myself into believing the stars are below me, instead of above.

I've never been this high up before. Not outside, anyway. With all the tunnels connecting the buildings every few floors, there's not much need to step outside at all. In fact, all the balconies on these upper floors are restricted, even to my family.

Next only to being stranded outside the city gates in the Dead Zone, standing here now is literally the very last place I ever thought I'd be. But I only have one chance to get what I came for before my chip shows up on the Citizens Monitoring Grid . . . and I'm not going to miss it.

Unless I slip and plunge to a very messy death. But I'm trying not to think about that.

I grasp for the ledge to steady myself against a sudden gust of wind. As I crouch, shivering in my totally-inappropriate-for-the-situation dress, another gust whips through my hair, untangling it from the elaborate braid Grandmother spent so long on just this morning. That seems like a lifetime ago now.

My day began like every other in my fourteen years. The lights clicked on at exactly eight o'clock. My list of activities scrolled across the holo-screen that floats in the middle of my room, and my hands began to shake. Sometimes they go numb, or I feel like the walls are closing in and have to splash water on my face to relax. Every day my itinerary is a little different, depending on what my mother and teacher set up for me the night before. There is always school, always shopping, always etiquette class, and never, ever any free time.

Whenever I'm not scheduled for an activity, my duty is to follow closely at my mother's heels while she attends luncheons, charity balls, and political meetings, or is visited by all the top clothing designers, who flatter and charm her so she will select one of their outfits. As the wife of one of the highest officials in Prince John's royal cabinet, she must set a good example at all times. She must demonstrate loyalty to the government and possess a sharp intellect, but should never question the laws of the land. She is always the best-dressed woman in the room.

As my father's daughter, the same high standards are expected of me.

Ugh.

In the days before King Richard left on his mission to broker trade agreements in a nearby star system, things were different. Better. More fun. Without the grid, we were free to roam The City without being tracked all the time. Now people mostly stay within the few buildings where they live and work or go to school. Richard was kind. He told corny jokes, and he used to play peekaboo with me when he and my father took breaks from the important work of running our city. He was the first one to tell me that my voice has a soothing, melodic tone to it that people seem to like. Personally, I can't hear it.

Richard's younger brother, Prince John, is totally different. He's been in charge these last five years, and everyone is afraid to make one wrong move. To cross him is to lose your job or your home, or worst of all, be tossed into the Dead Zone, the area outside The City where there's only scorched earth and the memories of a time many centuries ago when something called *nature* thrived. Even though it would be treason to say it aloud, I secretly pray for the return of the king.

But back to this morning. I got out of bed and waited for my maid, Ivy, to come dress me and do my hair. I know at my age I am perfectly capable of doing these tasks myself, but I'd be late for my first activity every day if I had to make my own choices. Just the idea of picking out the right clothes sends me into a panic of indecision. Perhaps if I were given a chance to make even *one* of my own decisions, I'd be better at it. This is another thing I don't say.

Instead of Ivy showing up today, though, my grandmother came instead. This made me happy — Ivy is efficient and sweet, but caring for me is her job. Grandmother *chooses* to care, and that is a very different thing. Grandmother is the only person who wraps her arms around me and holds me tight. She is the only one who can see that sometimes

I'm just going through the motions of my life without actually living it.

At least, I *think* she can see that. Grandmother has lost her power of speech, so she can't tell me. She is not yet seventy, but her mind is muddled and she wanders off a few times a day. The only time I'm thankful for the grid is when we need it to find her. She never goes far, thankfully, and her movements are slow, except when she braids my hair. She comes alive then. She likes listening to me speak, so sometimes I'll recite a poem, or make up a story about what life must be like on planets other than ours. She is treated with the utmost respect due to my father's position, and no one cares if she wears the latest style.

This morning Grandmother outdid herself. She wove my long strands in and out, twisting them around with ribbons until they were a work of art. She topped it off with a silver headpiece — a half crown — that held a large green jewel in the middle. I imagine even grass and leaves weren't that bright, but of course I don't know for certain. I stared at my reflection in the mirror over my dressing table. Most likely the entire headpiece had been synthesized in one of the labs before they began focusing on making our food supply. But that made it no less beautiful, and only slightly less valuable than if it had come from the earth itself.

I ran my fingers gently over the large, multifaceted stone. If it *was* real, it would be the most precious and expensive item I own. And, due to all the shopping and gifts people give me in the hopes of getting close to my parents, I own a *lot* of things.

"Where did you get this, Grandmother?" I asked. "Was it yours?"

I didn't expect an answer and I didn't get one. She only smiled in that vague way she has and patted me on the shoulder. She pulled closed the cinch sack that held her ribbons and bows, and left.

I lifted the headpiece off and watched as the sunlight shone through the stone and sent light dancing on my wall. Up close I could see tiny holes that ran all the way through the jewel, making the streams of light even more mesmerizing. I could admire the design all day. Instead, I laid the gift carefully inside one of my top drawers. I didn't want to share it with the world. I have to share too much as it is.

Ivy arrived then to dress me in a fancy gown we'd picked up yesterday that made me long to return to my comfortable pajamas. She slid on my heels as she chattered about the latest gossip involving who was dating who, who had spent all their salary on the newest hovercar just to crash it a day later, and wasn't Prince John just the handsomest?

Yuck. As she is always up on all the goings-on in The City, my parents no doubt consider Ivy to be a good companion for me. But our conversations never get any deeper than this, and some days I fear I may starve from lack of stimulation. I put on my usual smile and let Ivy keep chattering while I ate breakfast.

Later, in etiquette class, I practiced perfect posture by walking with a couch cushion balanced on my head. Apparently I slouch more than someone of my high social standing is supposed to. The instructor told us that people used to put books on their heads instead of cushions. I saw a holo-pic of a book once in school, but I have a hard time picturing what it would feel like to hold one, let alone imagine one on my head. After the forests had been destroyed and no more paper could be produced, the Great Fire took what was left of the libraries and turned them to ash.

My schoolteacher almost never talks about history, because the government insists no one wants to hear about the wars that wiped out 90 percent of the planet's inhabitants, or all the mining that depleted Earth's resources and poisoned the oceans. No one but me, that is. It's as if they want us to believe that The City has always been exactly the way it is now, under Prince John's rule. Yes, we are free of crime (the grid assures us of that by keeping track of every citizen's whereabouts); free of starvation (the jelloid vitasquares the laboratories churn out daily keep us healthy and our bellies sated); and the Beautification Laws mean that our always sparkly clean skyscrapers are surrounded by flowers and trees and grass. But it is all a lie. If you touch the trees or flowers or grass, you'll find they are all made of foam.

Class today was history-free, as usual. We began by practicing handwriting on our tablets with our digi-pens for an hour. Over and over I wrote, in perfect cursive, *feed me feed me feed me.*

"Marian?" My teacher stood over my desk, catching me unaware as her eyes flitted across my screen. She clicked her tongue at me. "Did you skip breakfast today?"

I didn't know how to answer. How could I tell her that I meant my *brain* was hungry, not my stomach? So I only nodded. Eyebrows lifted across the room as kids began to murmur. No one ever misses a meal.

The teacher clicked her tongue at me again and tapped her finger on the timer embedded in the corner of my tablet.

"There," she said. "I've given you a twenty-minute pass. Go to the dining hall and get a vita-square to eat. This oversight will not happen again, I trust?"

I shook my head and slipped my tablet into my bag. Shaking, I hurried out of the room before she could change her mind. Or before *I* could. I stood outside the door. Should I go home? Our apartment was only three buildings away; I could make it through the tunnels and back in time. But how would I explain my presence to our household staff?

I could go down to the airship base and watch the ships take off. As a child I'd always loved the roar of the engines and admired the gentle grace of the ships as they flew off into space. I've never wanted to ride on one, though — that would be way too frightening. Starting in one's fourteenth year, a few students are selected to visit our sister planet, Earth Beta, to learn from their choices. (Apparently their choices weren't much different from ours, from what I've heard from returning students. They just ruined their planet in different ways.) As my high-ranking father's daughter, though, my place is with my feet firmly planted on this planet — one rule I'm actually grateful for.

A full five minutes passed before I dutifully turned toward the elevator. How could I even *think* of going somewhere other than where my teacher instructed?

The dining hall is ten floors up, and when the elevator doors opened, they revealed one long table, full of men having what I assumed at first was an early lunch. But then I realized who was holding court at the head of the table and quickly shrank back against the back of the elevator. Prince John and his inner cabinet, including my father, were celebrating something important because their plates were piled high WITH REAL FOOD! They couldn't all have birthdays today, could they? I know for a fact that my father's birthday was two months ago. They all shoveled beans and corn and rice in their mouths while the prince stood at the head of the table, holding up a glass of a liquid that wasn't see-through.

Luckily the elevator doors whooshed closed before anyone could notice my arrival. I stood there, heart pounding. I could still hear the prince's deep, rumbling voice through the doors.

"A toast!" he declared. "It is finally done. The people of our great city still believe their do-gooder of a king is off spreading peace in the galaxy and trying to broker trade agreements to bring us food and other natural resources. A noble cause, indeed!"

Some of the men laughed at that. I couldn't tell if my father was one of them.

The prince continued, "In nine more months, six years will have passed since my brother 'abandoned' his people, and I'll officially be declared king. All of you can expect large bonuses for your loyalty to me during this time."

Cheers rang out at this news.

My elevator still hadn't moved. I took a step closer to the doors. Through the crack I saw the prince hold up what looked like a small notebook. But could it really be one? A real notebook? With real paper? "I did not dare store this information on any of the interwebs," he said in a solemn voice, "so I've gone the old-fashioned way and written it down."

Everyone leaned forward. Prince John turned to face my father and held the tiny book out to him. I did not dare breathe.

"Patrick, we all know how Richard disrespected you by not appointing you second-in-command while he was king. I will not make that mistake. You shall continue to benefit from his absence. I know you will keep this information safe."

Ding!

Startled, I jumped before realizing it was only the elevator. Someone had called it from another floor. I only got one more glimpse of the group before I started to move back down. But that was enough. My father took the notebook and slid it into his briefcase. "I will indeed" were the last words I heard.

I pressed myself up against the back of the elevator as people got on and off, acknowledging them with a forced smile. What had I just heard? Our good and kind King Richard had been tricked somehow? Or are we the ones being deceived? Had he never even *left the planet*?

Perhaps we all should have been suspicious sooner. Five years really *is* a long time for a leader of a planet to be gone. My thoughts were bouncing around so fast my head hurt. I didn't know my father felt mistreated by Richard. I thought they'd been friends.

I passed through the afternoon in a daze. Shopping with Ivy was a blur of cars, shops, and dressing rooms. I think I came home with ten new pairs of shoes, but maybe they were hats. At dinner I watched my dad happily eat his allotment of four vita-squares and two glasses of water, wondering how he could possibly be hungry. (I also wondered if my mother knew about his other meal.) He didn't seem at all upset about Prince John's news. This made my heart sink. I barely tasted my already tasteless food, as I couldn't tear my eyes from his briefcase on the floor beside his chair. I couldn't help thinking that actual *paper* was in there! Had it made his briefcase heavy? What did it feel like to touch it?

After dinner I returned to my room and stared at myself in the mirror. I don't like admitting this, but I do that a lot. I am not vain (well, maybe a little), but if too much time goes by without seeing myself I feel disconnected and strange. Seeing my face now gave me comfort when everything was turning upside down.

Ding! I jumped again. My nerves were clearly frayed. This time the alert came from my tablet, still buried in my bag from school. The message was probably from a classmate with my homework assignment. I ignored it. The tablet dinged twice more before I gave in and grabbed it.

But the message wasn't from a classmate. Or if it was, they were masking their identity very well. After a long, encrypted series of letters and symbols, the following words flashed on my screen:

> *Marian Fitzwalter, these instructions will disappear in thirty seconds. Tonight at midnight, the grid will be off-line for exactly twenty-eight minutes. This will give you enough time to get over to your father's office building and retrieve a small brown notebook from his locked desk drawer. The key will be waiting for you, taped beneath the desk chair. Inside the notebook you will find one page with writing on it. You are to capture the contents with your digi-pen, and then neatly rip out the page of the notebook. On the next piece of paper, you will write the following letters and numbers, so memorize them well:*
>
> *RA 28h 31m 29.49400s*
> *DEC –90° 50' 03.3738"*
> *DIST 6.37 ly*

You will then bury your pen in the dirt by the tree outside Tower 42B, tear up the piece of paper, and rinse the shreds down the drain in the office bathroom. Many people have risked their lives for this. Do not let them down and do not speak of this to anyone.

I could not have been more surprised by these words if they'd jumped off the screen and bitten me in the face. I had time to read them once more before they faded into nothing and the screen turned black. All I could see was my own shocked expression in the reflection. My head swam as I tried to reason it out, but I couldn't. Nor could I disobey.

And that is why, five hours later, I am crouching here on the ledge outside my own father's office, buffeted by wind and rain, having snuck through six tunnels, dodged three couples out for late-night strolls, ran up four back stairwells, taken two freight elevators, slipped out an emergency door onto the roof, and climbed down the fire escape ladder to this ledge. I have never done even ONE of those things before.

I take a deep breath and prepare to drop down onto the balcony when the light switches on in the office and two men rush inside. I freeze and press myself lower onto the ledge until I'm almost lying down.

"Where do you think he hid it?" one man asks. I don't recognize the voice, or the bottom half of him that I can see, but I do not dare to lift my head higher.

"Don't know, don't care," the other replies. "We only need to ransack the place, make it look like someone was searching for it. When King Richard turns up dead, Prince John's hands will come up clean and he can blame his enemies."

"But he doesn't have any enemies," the first guy points out as he pushes over chairs and pulls out the few unlocked desk drawers. "None who'll admit to it, anyway."

"Hey, you know the old saying: 'An enemy is just a friend you haven't double-crossed yet!'"

The first guy booms with laughter, then stops. "We better watch our backs, then."

They flip a few more couch cushions, toss out the contents of the cabinets behind the desk, then leave, not bothering to switch off the light.

Aren't they worried about the grid finding them here? They wouldn't know it's temporarily turned off. As soon as the thought crosses my mind, I know the answer. They're not worried because Prince John has ultimate control over the grid.

I don't have time to dwell on the unfairness of it all, because I have four more minutes until the grid turns back on. There is no chance at all that I can follow the instructions and make it back home in time. I will be caught for sure.

Is this whole insane mission a trap? Maybe I'm no different than those men, brought here as part of the prince's plan to frame his enemies. Maybe I'm being set up to take the fall. Or my father is.

Three minutes left. I have a big decision to make. Whoever sent me here must not know me well. They have left me no choice. I take a deep, ragged breath.

And jump.

CHAPTER THREE

↞ Robin ↠

Judging by the horrid taste of the broccoli-flavored vitasquare that the food replicator spewed out for dinner today, the original vegetable must have been barely edible. I would spit it out in protest, but I need all the energy I can get right now. I have a mystery to solve.

I have to admit, with the arrival of the mysterious boxes, the feather now tucked safely under my mattress, and Roboteach's bizarre photograph, this is turning into an exciting day. Usually the most exciting things that happen up here are an occasional spontaneous dance party in the plaza, or maybe a newbie to the station will get claustrophobic and run around in circles shouting *"GET ME OUT OF HERE!"* at the top of their lungs. But that's rare. Mostly we make our own fun and don't have too many rules to follow. My only real responsibility is attending school and not breaking anything. This leaves plenty of time for other pursuits.

All around me my classmates are still buzzing over the resemblance between the guy in the dorky hat and me. I pretend that it's just a coincidence, matching DNA or not. I don't want people to think it bothers me.

"How about a magic trick?" I ask, knowing that will get people off my case. I've been working on a new one, and this is as good a time as any to try it out. I slip my hand in my pocket and hide a round glass disk in my palm.

Gabriella leans across the table eagerly.

"Anyone have a token?" I ask.

"That depends," Toby says. "Will we get it back?"

I grin. "Can't promise that."

Gabriella digs into her pocket anyway and eagerly hands over what must be her last token.

"Why do you keep falling for this?" Finley asks her.

I generally stay away from Finley, even though he's closest to me in age. He's the commander's son and a bit of a buzzkill.

I drape my napkin (really an old piece of cloth that doubles as a napkin) over my empty water glass, then hold up Gabriella's token so everyone can clearly see it. I slide it under the napkin and wait for the clink it makes as it hits the bottom of the glass. Only the token is still in my hand — the clink was really the clear glass disk I had hidden in my palm. The disk fits exactly into the bottom of the glass, totally blending in so it's invisible. I snap my fingers and whisk away the cloth, revealing what looks like an empty glass and an empty napkin. Where'd the token go?

Everyone claps and hoots. Gabriella is so delighted she doesn't even complain about losing her token. While everyone is oohing and aahing over the seemingly empty glass, I ball up the napkin with the token that I'd never actually let go of and stick it all in my pocket.

Finley rolls his eyes, and that's my signal to leave. Quick as a flash, I flip the disk out of the glass and make a mental note of slight adjustments to make the next time I perform the trick. Then I hop on my board and zoom out of the dining hall. I may be able to fool the others into thinking I don't care about that photograph, but I'm having a hard time fooling myself. I have questions, and I know just the person to ask for answers.

With so few of us living in such a confined space, you learn to tell each person apart by the oddest traits. Like right now, I can tell that Will is trailing about twenty feet behind me because when he exhales, a faint whistle zips through his front teeth. It's so perfectly even that I swear you could use it to tell time. When I was younger, the rhythmic *huuh-huuh-fweee, huuh-huuh-fweee* used to lull me to sleep. Now between his whistling and Toby's singing, it's a wonder I get any sleep at all.

I pretend I don't know he's following me as I speed up, looping around the winding hallway that leads down to the lower level of the station.

Uncle Kent can usually be found in one of three places: Either he's playing cards in the back of Shane's garage, he's at his job monitoring the gravity generator, or he's staring out into the darkness of space on the Central Plaza's observation deck.

Since by all rights he *should* be in the middle of his shift at work right now, that means he's either playing cards at Shane's or on the deck. I head to the Central Plaza first. My lack of faith in my uncle's work ethic is rewarded when I easily spot the back of his head.

The glass dome that houses the observation deck extends fifty yards out into space. It totally gives the illusion of being outside, as long as you don't look behind you. Five rows of benches are permanently affixed to the transparent floor, but often people bring their own comfortable chairs, or even blankets. Uncle Kent is sitting in the first row, hands on his knees, face tilted up as he looks out into the cosmos. I plop down beside him. A few seconds later Will joins us.

It's time to find out what he knows.

"I don't know anything," Uncle Kent swears when I ask him who my parents are.

I shake my head. "C'mon, Uncle K. You've raised me like a son for fourteen years, and I don't even know if you're my mother's brother or my father's brother."

Uncle Kent rubs his forehead, adjusts the collar of his maintenance uniform, closes his eyes, then opens them again. "Honestly, Robin," he says wearily, "all of that is ancient history. Why does it matter all of a sudden?"

I tell him about the mystery man we saw in class, leaving out the part about the feather. I kinda want the feather to be just mine. Even though the kids in class know, of course, so it's not much of a secret anymore.

"Do you know who it could have been?" I ask.

He shakes his head. "You said there were trees? Real ones?"

Will and I nod.

"Whoever he was, he would have lived hundreds of years ago. What's the point in even thinking about it?"

He has a point. "All right, at least tell me the easy part, then." I gesture to the three of us on the bench. "Tell me how we're related."

He sighs, fixes his eyes out into the distance, and says, "We're not."

After a pause that seems to encompass months and years, Will and I both shout, "WHAT?"

I follow that up with "Sorry, come again?"

Uncle (?) Kent says, "Your parents were my best friends. When they left, I took you in. Will was just a baby, and his own mother was gone. I figured he could use an older brother. You were a little more than a year old at the time we all came here."

I try to process this. Did I live somewhere else before I lived here? Is that possible? "I don't understand, Uncle Kent — or should I just call you Kent now?"

He cringes at that. "Your father and I thought of each other as brothers. I was always your uncle, even if not by blood. And I always will be. We're a family."

"But where are my parents? What happened to them? You said they . . . left?" The idea that they willingly abandoned me had never occurred to me before, although it should have, of course. In this age of interplanetary travel, stories of people taking off for the hope of a better life elsewhere weren't unheard of. That's probably how half the people on Delta Z wound up here. They'd been left behind. Or were the ones doing the leaving.

Uncle Kent (guess that's how I'll always think of him) stands up and walks to the edge of the dome. "It's complicated," he says. "They didn't expect to be gone this long. Their mission was only supposed to last a year, two at the most."

Will and I hurry to join him at the window. "Mission?" I repeat. "What does *that* mean?"

"Were Robin's parents spies?" Will asks excitedly.

Uncle Kent gives a small smile, his first since we sat down. "Nothing that dramatic. But they did have an important job to do, one that was not wholly without risk. I just thought they'd be back by now and we'd all go home."

I follow his gaze out the window. I've never understood why he spends so many hours looking outside. We're so high in orbit that we can't see anything interesting, like the sunrises or sunsets people who live on the planet below get to see when they look out. All we can see are the stars zooming by in the distance as we get dragged around the planet like an afterthought. Frankly, it makes me dizzy if I look too long.

"Is that why you sit here and look out all the time?" I ask. "Are you waiting for them to return?"

He rubs his eyes again. "I suppose so."

Suddenly serious again, Will says, "So Delta Z isn't really our home?"

"Of course it is," Uncle Kent is quick to reply. I can hear him trying to keep his voice steady. "We've made a life here. It's a good one, isn't it?"

Will and I both nod. I'm sure Will's thoughts are spinning as much as mine. Has Uncle Kent stayed here all these years because of *me*? An unfamiliar feeling wells up inside me. *Gratitude*, I think they call it. And also sadness. What did he leave behind? What did he give up?

"I haven't given up hope of seeing them again," Uncle Kent continues, using almost the same words I'd been thinking. "The Locksley men are tough. If there's a way to —"

My hand shoots out to grab his arm. "What did you say? The *Locksley* men? What does that mean?"

"That's the town your parents came from. I grew up in the next town over."

While I try to process this, he adds, "Locksley men were known for their bravery. Always fighting for one cause or another. Stubborn, too."

"Locksley boxes," I stammer. "Boxes arrived from a ship."

"What?" Uncle Kent asks, finally meeting my eyes for the first time during this whole conversation.

I try again, and this time I make more sense. "A whole

bunch of boxes arrived that have *Property of Locksley Manor* printed on them."

His face pales. "When?"

"Just a few hours ago."

"Are you sure that's what they said?"

I nod as another unfamiliar feeling creeps in. *Worry.* I don't like it. It makes me itchy.

Uncle Kent stumbles back onto the bench and puts his face in his hands.

"Dad?" Will asks, his voice trembling. "What is it? What's wrong?"

"They're not coming back," he says, his voice barely above a whisper. "They knew what they were doing was dangerous, but they're really gone."

CHAPTER FOUR

Marian

Sloshing water all over the office floor as I step through the (thankfully unlocked) sliding glass door is the last thing I should be worrying about, but I still feel guilty. The housekeeping staff works hard to keep The City clean and neat. I reach down to rub my sore knees. They'd gotten scraped up when I jumped from the ledge to the balcony. Athletic activity is frowned upon at our social level, and now I see why. It hurts!

My father used to bring me up here all the time when I was little, in the days of King Richard, but not once since. The office feels less inviting now, and colder, and not only because I'm shivering from the rain.

I run over to the office chair — or what's left of it, anyway. Where is the key? I fall to my knees (ouch) and crawl around the floor, feeling around for it. In a city without crime, why would he have moved it?

I scramble back up and feel around the desk. All the drawers are hanging open except for the locked one at the top, where the notebook is. I tug at it, but it doesn't budge. Still, I tug again and feel around the edges to see if I can wedge something in, but it's solid.

Two minutes. My mouth has gone completely dry. Maybe I can bang something against it until the drawer breaks apart. I push my hair away from my face and look around the room, willing a solution to come to me. What about the bust of Prince John that he had installed in everyone's offices? I wouldn't mind smashing *that* thing. But besides the noise that would cause, I can feel the thickness of it. I could toss it over the balcony and it likely wouldn't break.

My eyes then land on the holo-pic of our family, on the wall beside the door. The intruders knocked it sideways, but it still hangs from one bracket. The royal photographers took it years ago at a banquet when my father received an honor from King Richard for something or other. I risk a small smile at the image of Grandmother, whose eyes are a little more focused than they are now. We're all smiling in the image, too. I remember it was a special night, with dancing and music.

I reach out to straighten the holo-pic. But when I try to snap it back onto the bracket, it bulges a little in the center. I reach behind it and feel a lump.

My hand stops, and then I yank the whole picture off the wall. The notebook is attached to the thin holo-screen with clear tape. I scratch and pull at it until it springs free.

I'm out of time now, but I keep going. I'm nothing if not a rule follower. The notebook is much lighter than I thought it would be, barely weighing anything. I'm not sure what good this would do on someone's head.

I flip it open and have to stop myself from running my hands over the soft, delicate pages. Most are blank; one reveals three lines of code in gray lettering:

RA 14h 39m 36.49400s
DEC –60° 50' 02.3737"
DIST 4.37 ly

I should be focusing on what those numbers might mean, or how they would lead someone to Richard, but all I can do is marvel at it. I run my finger gently over the letters and numbers, and I can feel the slight indentations in the page left by the writing tool that made them. Pens holding ink and pencils with lead or graphite do not exist anymore, of course, so whoever wrote this must have gotten creative.

Closing my eyes doesn't make ripping out the piece of paper any easier. It feels so destructive, like ripping off someone's limb. The tearing sound that it makes will haunt me. But I pull out my digi-pen, scan the document, and tuck it safely back in my belt.

Any second now that door will burst open. I should get rid of the evidence, as instructed. I should go rinse it down the sink. But I can't, I just can't. I stick the paper into my boot, and then my stomach twists as I turn back to the notebook. I don't have anything to write with! How am I supposed to enter in the false codes? Why hadn't whoever wrote me the letter considered this?

And why hasn't the door opened by now with Prince John's guards storming in?

I try to remember if I learned anything in school about making a writing tool, but such lessons are painfully few and far between. I need something brown or black that I can mix with water, or even saliva.

I need to burn something to get ash. But what? Everything is made to last forever now. Parts don't rub off or break or splinter or burn. My dress is inflammable, as are the curtains and rug and everything else in the entire city. Then I glance down at the notebook. I am holding perhaps the only thing on the planet that can still burn. I can't bring myself to rip out another piece, so, reluctantly, I pull out the paper with the code and tear off the bottom half. The sound is just as painful this time.

I turn my digi-pen to the maximum heat setting, the one reserved only for emergencies, and focus the beam on the paper in my hand.

I realize a second too late how stupid that was, as the heat instantly burns a hole clear through the paper and keeps going. I yelp as my palm turns red and the skin actually *sizzles*. I ball up the wet hem of my dress and clutch it in my palm to ease the pain. A second later, though, the pain is gone. The medi-bots in my cells have done their job. I unclench my fist. The red spot has completely faded away.

More carefully this time, I burn the paper until I get a pile of ash big enough. I wring out a few drops of water from my dress and stir. Using the tip of my fingernail, I try not shake too much as I copy the code from the letter. The color is darker than the original ink, and the ash smears a bit on the page, but it will have to do. I'm not entirely certain that I got all the numbers and letters correct, either.

I calmly tape the notebook back in place, already missing the feel of it in my hands. There's no longer a reason to hurry. Or to sneak out the back.

So I walk straight out the door into the dark, empty hall, fully expecting a guard to jump out before I make it to the elevator. But no one does. Odd. I keep going. No one is in the elevator, either. I consider taking it to the first tunnel, then the second, but I let the elevator continue to descend until I'm on the ground floor. I haven't been alone on the surface in years. Maybe ever.

As I step out into the stagnant night air, now misty from the rain, it's all I can do not to laugh. This is absurd! The lights of the few hovercars nearby twinkle only a few yards above my head. If I didn't know better, I'd say I had to be dreaming. But my dreams are always scattered things, snippets of scenes from the brain-numbing events I'd been made to sit through that day. I couldn't possibly have dreamt up a night like this.

Then again . . . there is the pesky matter that no one has come to arrest me for theft, or even stopped me for sneaking around in the middle of the night where I don't belong. I straighten my dress and grin. I'm just going to *pretend* it's a dream and finish out the mission. Otherwise the fear will overtake me. I walk down the dark streets toward the spot where I'm supposed to drop off my digi-pen, grinning like a fool. Unbelievably, I spot the same strolling couple that I saw earlier in one of the tunnels and give them a wave. They wave back. They are friendly dream people. Not like the ransackers. They weren't nice at all.

I may be losing my mind, but I'm so very tired. I've never been awake for this many hours in a row. It's messing with my brain.

I soon reach the fake tree and take a minute to delete all my personal data. Every image I've ever snapped, every song I've sang, everything I've ever written for school, even *feed me feed me feed me* is recorded in there. I blink back tears. Even though my life isn't what I'd hoped it would be, it's still mine.

And now it's all gone, leaving only the scanned code from the notebook page. I bury the pen in the fake soil and cover it up. Wiping my hands on my torn, wet mess of a dress, I turn toward home. I've made it two blocks when I see Grandmother, of all people, absently strolling down the opposite side of the street.

She looks up as I rush over to her. I've never known her to wander down here before, certainly not in the dead of night, but of course I'm always asleep at this time. Her squished-up forehead relaxes as soon as she sees me. "Let's go home, Grandmother," I tell her in my most soothing, relaxed voice. It surprises me to hear it after so many hours of speaking to no one. She links her arm through mine and squeezes.

So she won't be scared, I chat as we walk, sharing the gossip from Ivy, joking about the lovely sunny day. We're in front of our building when a bright light shines directly in my face and we freeze. My hand flies up to protect my eyes. "Marian Fitzwalter," a guard's voice says, checking a screen in one hand, no doubt looking at the grid for my name. "I'm going to have to bring you in for breaking curfew."

My mouth goes instantly dry. Before I can choke out a word, the guard swings the light over to Grandmother, who continues to look calmly ahead. He drops the light almost immediately.

"Oh, excuse me, ma'am. I didn't realize it was you."

Grandmother waves her hand and gives him a small, patient nod like you would to a child who has tracked fake dirt on the rug. The guard steps aside and we enter. I'm shaking so badly I'm not sure if I'm the one leading Grandmother up to our apartment, or if she's leading me.

When I wake up in the morning my wet, torn dress is gone, and Ivy is her usual chirpy self as she dresses me for the day. I only catch a few words, as my head is swirling with the events of the night. I absently rub the center of my palm. My brain can remember the searing pain as it burned, but it's as smooth as it ever was. I'm so, so very tired, though. All I want to do is crawl back to bed.

But of course my full schedule forbids that. When Ivy leaves me to gather my things, I check my tablet and am relieved to find no follow-up message and no trace of the one from yesterday. I shake my head. It's almost too easy to believe it really *was* a dream.

It doesn't take long to rid me of that notion. I arrive for breakfast to find my mother still in her bathrobe, a sight I haven't seen since I was four years old and she was having a bad hair day and refused to leave our apartment until the finest hairdresser in The City arrived.

"But who *did* this?" my mother shrieks across the table at my father. "Who could just go in your office and destroy it? Isn't this what the grid is supposed to protect against?"

"Apparently there was a malfunction," my father replies, rubbing his forehead. "It has never happened before."

"What about the surveillance cameras?" she asks.

My lungs literally stop the intake of air. Surveillance cameras! I hadn't even thought of such a thing!

"They were down, too," he says. "All over the city."

I resume breathing while she shakes her head.

"Unbelievable. Was anything . . . *stolen*?" She says the word like it's too insane a concept to consider.

He shakes his head. "Not that I could see when security called me earlier. Housekeeping has already straightened up."

"Well, whoever did this must have been looking for *something*."

My father hesitates only for a split second before he stops pacing and shrugs. "Probably just kids letting off steam."

I know it wasn't kids. He probably knows it, too, but it's always best to avoid feeding into Mother's dramatic nature.

It seems I've escaped detection. My sigh of relief must be audible, because they finally notice me standing there. My mother pushes my plate across the counter toward me.

Father plants a kiss on my cheek. "Don't worry about all this," he says. "It's just grown-up stuff. It's all taken care of."

Inside I'm screaming, *This is your fault. You're siding with the enemy.* But I just nod and eat my vita-squares. I think they're supposed to taste like eggs and bacon, but I really couldn't say.

My first stop after breakfast is a clothing designer's studio, where two women gush over me and I actually let them. I start giggling when they measure my waist — and I am *not* a giggler. But I'm feeling pretty good now. Almost giddy. If what I did will help King Richard somehow, it was worth the risk.

"So, is there a special guy?" one of the women teases while the other finishes sewing a skirt they made me. "You have such a lovely voice. I bet all the boys are in love with you."

I shake my head. This question used to embarrass me, but now I don't mind. Most of the other kids in my social circle are paired up, mostly thanks to their parents' meddling. But to my mother's credit, she has never rushed me in that department. Four boys in my class are possible contenders, but when it comes down to picking which one, it won't be my choice. I've honestly never given it much thought.

It's interesting watching the designers work. They obviously enjoy creating their clothes. In the hour that we've been here, they've transformed a flat piece of cloth into a stylish skirt, scarf, and gloves. They've even added a belt to Ivy's maid uniform. I laugh as she turns in circles in front of the mirror, admiring her new shape.

When I walk into my classroom, in a better mood than I've probably been in years, everyone stops talking. It takes me a few seconds to register the hush that has now fallen has to do with me. I stop before I reach my desk and look around. Every single student is watching me. Their expressions are not unkind — well, most of them aren't — but I keep a low profile in school, so this type of attention is totally unusual. Unless . . .

Unless they know about last night! What if everyone in the class got that letter, and I was the only one crazy enough to obey? Maybe it was some kind of elaborate joke that everyone was in on except for me? Did someone find the scrap of paper hidden deep in the toe of my boot?

Do I run out of the room? Do I play dumb?

While I'm frozen with indecision, a girl named Sarena, who is in a lower social class but has always been nice to me, jumps up from her chair. She lunges toward me and throws her arms around my neck.

I stumble back in surprise and almost fall across my desk. I untangle myself and step away. "What's going on, Sarena?" I ask.

"Haven't you heard?" she says.

I hesitate, then shake my head. Guess I'm going with the "play dumb" strategy.

Eyes sparkling, Sarena exclaims, "You were picked to go to Earth Beta! I was, too! We'll get to go together!"

My eyes widen. This is truly the last thing I am expecting to hear. It can't be right. So I ask her to repeat it.

"We're going on an airship!" she squeals. "You, me, Asher, and Gareth!"

I shake my head as my stomach flips over. My parents will never allow this. "It must be a mistake," I say weakly.

My teacher points to a list of names posted on the holoscreen tethered to the front of the classroom. My name is definitely on it. And next to my name are my parents' signatures. Both of them. But they know I've never wanted to leave the planet. Not that it was ever an option before — or at least, I'd always been told it wasn't. Asher and Gareth are also in a lower social class, roughly equal to Sarena's. I don't know either of them too well — Asher is tall, pale, and blond, and I know a lot of the girls have crushes on him. Gareth has black hair that he wears long and pulled back. He's good at math and quiet, while Asher talks enough for the both of them, always wanting to prove how much he knows about everything.

I glance at my classmates and finally recognize the expression on their faces: jealousy. And, on a few, suspicion. I'm not the only one who believed that kids of government officials don't go off-world.

Because of that, I've never paid any attention to the selection process, or even bothered to pay attention to when it took place, but some kids have been waiting all year for the announcement. I didn't even realize it was today. People have been sucking up to the council for years to get these four coveted spots.

The teacher announces to the room, "Usually we wait a few more months for the announcement, but the council has decided to send the next group early this year. Marian, Asher, Gareth, and Sarena, you will be dismissed from class today to pack and say your goodbyes. You leave tomorrow."

Loud murmuring rings out from the class, joined by gasps from the four of us.

"So soon?" Asher asks, standing up from his seat. "Don't we need time to train?"

"You're fast learners," the teacher snaps. "You'll pick it up as you go along."

The others are already hugging classmates and gathering their supplies. I know I should be grateful that the incident at my father's office has gone unmentioned — or most likely was covered up — but it's hard to focus on that right now. I lick my lips nervously and whisper to the teacher, "Maybe someone else can go in my place?"

She leans toward me and, through gritted teeth, replies in a kinder voice than she's ever used with me, "This is an opportunity of a lifetime, Marian. Don't blow it."

CHAPTER FIVE

↢ Robin ↣

It's hard to be upset when you're flying through the air while your not-blood-related cousin aims vita-squares at your mouth.

Uncle Kent, Will, and I have all reacted differently to yesterday's revelations. Will spent the rest of yesterday and most of this morning looking like someone just tossed his hoverboard out into the vacuum of space. I repeatedly tried to convince him that he will always be my cousin — and my best friend — no matter what. I don't think he fully believed me until I did something I'd vowed never to do, something that goes against the magician's unspoken code: I revealed how I always know what card he's going to pick when I do a card trick. It was a bold move, but I knew I had to go big. It worked, so it was worth it.

As for Uncle Kent, he essentially abandoned his post after I told him about the boxes. This means that whenever it's Uncle Kent's shift, everyone and everything who isn't strapped or bolted down is spending a lot of time in the air. The commander (who is normally a pretty decent guy) warned him that if he doesn't leave the back of Shane's garage in the next fifteen minutes he's going to lose his job. Will and I are flying/swimming there now to try to convince him to go. It's a slow way to travel, but our hoverboards don't work in zero-g, so we have to make the best of it, grabbing onto walls to propel ourselves along.

And as for me, I sat alone on that bench on the observation deck for hours after Will and Uncle Kent went back home. My emotions were all over the place, which is not how I like them to be. First learning I had parents in the first place, then finding out only moments later that I didn't have them anymore. That would mess with anyone.

"Robin!" Will calls back to me as we enter the front of the shop. "You swing your left leg down and I'll use it to catapult myself over the top of the shelves."

I do as I'm told, and he flings himself over the shelves and does a perfect in-air somersault. His high-jump skills come in handy in zero-g. He lands right above the table, which, like all the furniture at the station, is nailed to the ground. I follow soon after, but not nearly as gracefully.

The poker players are strapped into their chairs, and they've rigged up these nets over their cards and chips. It's pretty clever, actually. Not much would make these guys call off a game.

"Dad!" Will shouts. "You've got to stop giving away your paycheck. What if I want to go to college some day?"

The men (and one woman) around the table guffaw at that.

"Hey!" Will says, crossing his arms. "It could happen."

"I don't *always* lose," Uncle Kent mutters without looking away from his hand.

He's clearly not budging. All we can do is watch until the game is over and try to reason with him then. The playing cards are spinning into the nets quickly, clinking as they hit one another. Shane's managed to build up quite a collection, all from mismatched decks. If a pilot on one of the transport ships wants to be dealt into a game, he or she has to pony up something of value. They all know Shane needs cards, so they stock up for when they come here. The cards are all made out of plastic, of course, which makes them very sturdy. I once did a project for school on the history of playing cards and was surprised to know that they were once made out of paper and cardboard, which sounds very flimsy to me.

Beep beep buzzzz. There go the sirens! That means the next shift is about to begin. Will and I hook onto the backs of the players' chairs with our feet and slide ourselves to the ground. A few seconds later, the gravity generator turns back on and our bodies feel sluggish and heavy for a few minutes while we adjust. One time I ignored the sirens for a second too long and plunged to the ground. I won't make that mistake again.

When the game is over, I stand behind my uncle's chair and whisper, "I'm going to open the boxes now. Do you want to come or not?"

He doesn't answer at first, then pushes his chair back angrily. "I told you last night, I'm not ready."

"That was last night," I point out. "This is an entirely new day. I'm going."

He makes a noise that's a combination of a growl and a grunt. "Fine. We'll go together."

But when the three of us get to the cargo bay, the boxes aren't against the wall anymore. Uncle Kent gives me a skeptical look. "They were right here," I insist. "They must have moved them to one of the storage rooms."

But the storage rooms are empty, too, except for three rubber tires and a bag of nails. It's been a slow few days at the station.

I throw up my arms. "Where'd they go?"

We head back into the main cargo bay just as Vinnie comes in from the other end. He sees Uncle Kent first and scowls.

"I'm getting real sick of the zero-g." He points his finger at Uncle Kent's chest. "If you don't like your job, find another one. Life's too short and I'm tired of wasting mine on the ceiling." Then he spots me and Will, and his face darkens even more. "Shouldn't you both be in school?"

Uncle Kent swats the foreman's hand away. "Just a minute, Vincent."

Vinnie scowls again. He hates being called his full name. Will and I stifle a laugh.

Uncle Kent steps in front of us. "We're trying to find a stack of boxes that arrived yesterday. Said *Property of Locksley Manor* on them. I believe they belong to me."

The foreman shakes his head. "Do you see any boxes?"

To his credit, Uncle Kent doesn't give him the satisfaction of looking around the empty room.

"They were up against the wall in the main cargo bay," I add. "I saw them when I was here yesterday, remember?"

Vinnie shrugs. "We must have gotten ten deliveries and pickups since then. They're obviously gone." He shoos us out the door. "I know you all have better places to be. And one of you should probably start looking for a new job!" The door slams behind us.

"Now what?" I ask. "I haven't seen any more ships arrive since yesterday. Have either of you?"

They both shake their heads.

"He knows something," my uncle says. "All that poker playing has given me a pretty good knack for knowing when someone is lying."

"Why would he lie about boxes?" Will asks.

Uncle Kent shakes his head. "I don't know, but I'm going to find out. All arrivals and departures are logged into a database, including a record of their cargo. I'll start there. You two go to school, and I'll catch up with you later."

I hesitate, sort of feeling like I should be part of this. After all, the packages have more to do with me than anyone else.

Before I can say anything, Uncle Kent shakes his head. "No. You're obviously not the foreman's favorite person."

I raise my chin. "Neither are you, remember? You keep making everyone float!"

"Vinnie and I go way back. I know how to talk to him. Now get to school before you're late again and then complain about being stuck in waste disposal for a week."

Okay, the man has a good point. I'm lucky I'm not down there already. "Good luck," I tell him. "If you find the boxes, don't open them until I get there."

"Wouldn't dream of it," Uncle Kent says. I look back to see him square his shoulders and knock on the door.

Will and I slide into our seats about ten seconds before the afternoon buzzer rings. I'm relieved to see that Roboteach has laid out two pieces of brown fabric on our desks with small lines marked on them. A new sewing project. Much better than another discussion about DNA and ancient history.

Those of us old enough to wield a needle without impaling ourselves upon it have been sewing for years. With our limited access to new clothes, everyone needs to learn this skill. Today I'm glad for the mindlessness of the lesson. I can follow the lines with my needle and thread while letting my mind wander to more pressing things. He's a good man, my uncle. This can't be easy for him. He'd probably rather believe the foreman, since it would mean he could pretend the boxes never came, and my parents are still alive. But there he went, knocking on that door. I'm lucky to have him. Better than parents who would abandon their kid and then get themselves killed.

"Ouch!" My squeal comes out sounding a little more like a six-year-old girl's than I would like. I immediately press my finger to my lips to stop the drip of blood.

"Do you need to visit the medi-station, Robin?" Robo-teach asks, wheeling over to me.

I shake my head.

"Good!" He spins back around. "All right, class, let's all set our hats aside and get ready for the next activity. You're going to like this one."

Hats? I look down at the fabric in my hand. Brown. Triangular. Soft. Then I glance around the class. Half the kids have already finished theirs and have plopped them on their heads. Pointy in the front, with sides that curve inward. It's the hat in the photograph!

Will laughs as he, too, sticks his hat on his head and beams. I just grumble. I don't think it's very funny. Everyone else is smiling, though. We never, ever get to wear hats up here. What would be the point? There's no sun to shield our eyes from.

"Hats off," Robo-teach repeats.

"Aw," the girls complain, grabbing them off one another's heads and giggling. I don't know if girls everywhere giggle a lot, but our girls sure do. Once I heard two of them whispering, and when they saw me, they started giggling even more. Will says they have a crush on me, which is a weird way of saying they like me or think I'm cute or something. I've never had "a crush" on anyone so I don't really know what Will means. Uncle Kent says someday I'll meet my "person" and then I'll understand. I've seen Will get all gooey-eyed when he talks to Malaya, who is only a month older than him, but I don't really get it. I finish the last few stitches and tie off the thread.

"Now," Robo-teach continues, "I will be pairing you up by age for this next project." Half the class hoots (including Will, who will get to pair up with Malaya), the other half groans (that'd be me, since it means I get to spend close-up and personal time with Finley).

"Since everyone was so interested in the DNA process yesterday, we're going to dive in a little deeper. I've downloaded my processing program onto the mobile viewscreens. You will each take turns collecting a hair sample from your partner, give it to me to upload, and then return to your seats to watch the results."

Everyone hurries to switch seats to be closest to their partner, but I drag my feet. I'm not in any hurry to see that guy's face again. And what if the experiment pulls up something about my parents? I'm pretty sure I couldn't handle that.

"Ouch!" I squeal for the second time in ten minutes. "Seriously, Finley? That hurt!" I furiously rub the spot on my head where he just yanked out more than one piece of my hair. In response, he calmly pulls out one single strand of his own hair and says, "Saved you the trouble." Then he delivers them both to Robo-teach.

Grumbling, I plop down in front of our viewscreen to wait. Across the room, little Lissy shouts, "I'm related to a queen! I knew it!"

By the time Finley returns, his data is starting to fill the screen. "I already know my family tree dating back three hundred years," he brags, leaning back in his chair.

This doesn't surprise me. The commander prides himself on being the latest in a line of leaders (commanders, captains, chiefs, kings, presidents, you name it) going back fifteen generations or something. He and Finley's mother are the first people to pop up on the screen, then lots of other faces, places, and documents. Finley's barely paying attention until . . .

He and I both lean forward.

It looks like . . .

He suddenly lunges forward and flips the viewscreen over. His face has gone very red. I don't blame him. I'd be pretty embarrassed to find out my great-great-great-grandfather was a thief with a million-dollar bounty on his head.

Actually, I probably wouldn't care. But Finley obviously does.

"Please," he gasps, stabbing at the screen with his fingers until it goes dark. "Don't tell anyone."

I consider this for a minute. Having something to hold over Finley could be useful. But he looks so distressed that I just shrug and say, "Sure, whatever."

"Thank you," he says, his cheeks still flaming. "I owe you one."

Robo-teach wheels up to our table. "Find anything interesting, boys?"

Finley opens his mouth, then quickly shakes his head.

"Nope," I say, "just Finley's family history of do-gooders."

Robo-teach nods. "I'm sure you'll be as good a commander as your father one day."

Finley gives a quick nod and stares at his hands.

"What about you, Robin?" Robo-teach asks. "Have you been able to shed any light on your mysterious look-alike?"

"Haven't checked yet." I turn the screen toward me and flick it back on. I can't help noticing that next to Finley's first name is his last name, Harlon. But mine only says Robin. Why have I never thought about that before?

I take a deep breath and press on my name. I expect the photograph to come right up again, but it doesn't. Only four words appear on the screen:

NO MATCHES ON FILE.

I try again. Same message comes up.

"How is that possible?" I ask Robo-teach. He shakes his head and starts scanning his own data from yesterday with the feather, but instead of pulling up the photograph, the same error message flashes across his screen.

"I'm sorry, Robin," he says, in as sorry a tone as a robot can muster. "All traces of your family history appear to have been wiped."

CHAPTER SIX

Marian

With my teacher's warning ringing in my ears, I stumble my way out of the classroom. That couch cushion would have fallen right off my head as I hurry through the halls, half bent over, trying to make myself disappear. I can't go into space! That's absurd! No one knows how long it goes on, maybe forever! Sarena calls after me, but I keep moving until she gives up.

I burst into our apartment calling my mother's name. No one answers, not Grandmother or even the staff. My parents must have given them the day off while they deal with the office break-in. I pull up the picture of my mother's face on my tablet. Her "do not call" button is lit up. I call anyway. A few seconds later, her face appears on the screen, covered in a clay mask with holes for her eyes, nose, and mouth. I've interrupted her weekly facial. I can live with that.

Before she can say anything, I jump in. "Mother! There's been a mistake. You have to fix it. I was chosen to go to Earth Beta!"

Calmly, she says, "Yes, I know. I think it will be good for you. You've been slacking lately on your studies."

"Not true," I argue, heat rising to my cheeks. "My grades are fine."

"I don't mean in school," she says, the clay cracking around her lips as she talks. "I mean in all the other ways a young lady in your position should act. Ivy will return shortly to help you pack, and she will accompany you on the journey. You're representing our family now, so I expect you to be on your best behavior while you're gone."

This is crazy! "When am I ever *not* on my best behavior?"

She closes her eyes as someone out of frame drapes a wet washcloth across her face. "Right now," she replies calmly.

AHHHHH! I shut off the screen, stomp around a bit, then sink into the couch. Fine. If they want me to go so badly, I'll go. I stomp to my room, aware that stomping in high heels looks ridiculous. I kick them into my closet and take a good look around my room. I've never lived anywhere other than here. I've never even slept in any bed other than this one. Except for a cradle, of course, and that hardly counts.

Ivy runs in with two suitcases, one big and one small. She leaves the small one by the door and plops the big one on my bed. "We are going to have the best time!" she exclaims.

It takes me a few seconds to remember that my mother said Ivy would be coming with me. Well, it's a relief at least to know that *someone* will be looking out for me.

A bunch of instructions have arrived on both my holo-screen and tablet. It includes a strict packing list and information on liftoff. It really is tomorrow. I sit down on the bed and let Ivy fill my suitcase while rattling off all the exciting things we'll get to do and see on our trip.

"Where is your digi-pen?" she asks, looking around the desk for it. "That's number four on the list."

"I . . . um . . . lost it?"

"I will request a new one immediately." She types a few commands into her wrist device. One of the things I like about Ivy is how she never judges.

"I hear the boys are really cute on Earth Beta!" she says, neatly packing the high-heeled shoes I only recently kicked off. I lift them right back out. We play this game for a few more minutes before I just lie down and let her finish.

I must have fallen asleep, because when I open my eyes again, Ivy is gone and Grandmother is standing in my door frame. I spring up and run into her arms like I'm a child again. She holds me for a few minutes, making little murmuring sounds, which is the closest she can come to speech. Right now I'm not sure it's enough.

When I finally let go, she opens the top of my suitcase and looks around my room, puzzled. Then she points to the top of my head. It only takes a few seconds before I realize she's asking about the crown that she gave me yesterday. I shake my head. "I can't bring that. It's much too valuable and special. I wouldn't want to lose it."

But she keeps nodding and pointing, so I pull it out of the drawer to show her I'm keeping it safe there. She takes it from me and rests it on top of a dress that Ivy has folded with impossible neatness.

"Truly, Grandmother, I don't think I should bring it. What if someone on the other planet steals it? I'd feel awful."

She just zips up the suitcase as if I'm not even talking. Guess I'm bringing it.

* * *

The next day is one of those sunny days where your mood is so dark that the sun is an affront. It's poking fun at you by shining and making things glow like nothing bad could ever happen when you know it can.

Father's hovercar takes us to the launchpads where my three classmates are already gathered, along with their families. I'm the only one with her maid. The airship parked on the closest launchpad is so enormously huge that I literally cannot see the top of it. The *Royal Horizon* must be taller than any building in The City. I've seen a lot of ships before, but not one like this. I wonder if Prince John owns it, because of the name. Not that I've ever heard of him leaving the planet. The thought of it being able to lift off the ground boggles the mind.

The two men who will be our instructors for the three-month-long trip come over to introduce themselves. One glance tells me they are grandfather and grandson. White-haired Mr. Pratchett Senior is older than Grandmother, and Mr. Pratchett Junior ("call me PJ") is about ten years older than me, with a whistle on a chain around his neck. They make an odd pair. They go over the briefing that I already read last night, so I tune out.

PJ must say something funny because the group laughs, including my parents. Both of their moods have improved drastically since yesterday. Neither has mentioned my father's office again. Maybe they're just happy not to have anyone to take care of for a few months. That thought darkens my mood even further.

"We're going to say goodbye now," Father says as the group disbands. He puts his hands on my shoulders.

"You're not going to wait till the ship takes off?" I ask, incredulous.

He shakes his head. "It's better this way. I have to get back to work, and your mother has a —" I lift my brows, waiting for him to say she has something important, too, like getting her nails trimmed. He sighs. "Well, she has a thing. I'm sure it's vital to all of society."

I almost crack a smile at that. I've missed joking around with him. It feels like a distant memory. He gives me a hug, which feels both reassuring and awkward. He's both familiar and a stranger to me. Mother's hug is a little shorter. "You'll be back before you know it," she says.

My chest feels like a hovercar is sitting on it as I watch them go back to the parking lot. Ivy has stood silently beside me the whole time. For once she is quiet, and for once I wish she wouldn't be. Anything to keep my mind from whirling.

PJ blows his whistle, and it's time to go. It's a good thing Ivy is carrying both our suitcases, because my hands are shaking too much to hold them. The only thing giving me any comfort at all right now is the small scrap of paper in my left boot. Knowing that I have something that has survived for hundreds of years gives me hope somehow.

We file up the plank and into the cavernous opening of the ship. All of our jaws drop at the same time. I don't know what I expected to find, but the ship looks exactly like the interior of the buildings in the city: shining and clean, and laid out exactly the same as the main lobbies. Where's the creativity? Will there be an exact duplicate of our apartment, too?

While Mr. Pratchett Senior goes to tell the captain we're ready for takeoff (ugh), PJ points in two different directions, showing us where the boys' room will be, and where Sarena,

Ivy, and myself will be staying. He then tells us to step aside, that the door will now be closing.

We turn to watch as the door slides down from the top, soundlessly and with great finality as the outside world begins to shrink from our view. It's such a large opening that it takes longer than one might think. I catch another movement out of the corner of my eye. It's Ivy! She's heading purposefully toward the door!

I rush after her. "Ivy! What are you doing?"

"I'm not going on the trip," she says, patting my arm gently. "You don't need me here."

"I do!" I insist. "Please."

She shakes her head and pulls away from my grip. "Don't forget to brush your hair once in a while." She ducks out, right before the door clangs to the floor. It's pretty dramatic, really. I stand there, dumbfounded. Her parting words to me are about my hair? I sigh. I guess that's not surprising.

"So your robot maid left, eh?" Gareth says.

I turn to glare at him, but his kind expression tells me he isn't trying to be mean.

I nod.

"C'mon," he says. "I'll help you take your bags up to your room."

"I only have one," I tell him, pointing at the large suitcase. But then I notice the smaller version sitting beside it. I glance back at the huge door, but I know it's not going back up again. Ivy's gone. I sigh. Guess I have two. I hope there's nothing she needs in there.

I don't get more than four feet toward the elevator before a jolt runs up through the ground and sets my bones vibrating. "What was *that*?" Sarena asks in a trembling voice.

Asher grins. "Look!" He points to the wall — or at what *used* to be a solid wall. It's now completely transparent, as is the floor. My hands go numb as I spot The City below us, a perfect grid of gleaming, white towers surrounded by black, scorched earth in all directions. And then a second later it disappears, swallowed up by the glare of the sun, which we are moving toward — and now *past* — at an alarming rate.

My brain (and maybe my mouth, I'm not sure) screams *SHOULDN'T WE BE STRAPPED IN?* But the four of us are glued to the wall, pressing our hands and faces up against it as we approach a dark darker than any on Earth. A second later, we all draw in our breath and hold it. Outside the wall lies a view I will never, ever forget as long as I live. It's a sight that chases out all the fears and worries and all rational thought.

We are surrounded by STARS.

CHAPTER SEVEN

↢ Robin ↣

Since the sun doesn't rise or set over Delta Z, night and day are relative concepts. When he took over, the commander chose to align our noon and midnight with the planet below us. To tell the difference, all the lights dim at night, and are on full blaze during the day. Since I can't sleep due to my whole life apparently no longer existing, I've spent most of the last ten hours wandering the dark station and now the bright lights seem like a cruel joke. I'm currently shooting off virtual arrows into virtual targets because I can't deal with going to real-life school today, no matter the consequences.

"There you are, Robin!" Will says, running up behind me. "I've been looking all over for you. I haven't seen you for more than a few minutes since class yesterday."

"I'd have thought this would be the first place you'd check." *Swoosh!* I let an arrow fly. "Do you know I don't have a last name?"

"Huh?" Will asks as my arrow hits the virtual bull's-eye, as they almost all do. This game is probably rigged in favor of the player so we'll keep feeding it tokens.

"I don't have a last name," I repeat. "You're Will Stutely, Finley is Finley Harlon, Shane is Shane McAllister, and I'm Robin. Just Robin."

Will doesn't say anything for a minute, then blurts out, "Not so. You're Robin of Locksley!"

I consider his answer, then shake my head. "That's not a name; that's a place."

"Why can't it be both?"

"It doesn't matter anyway," I tell him, reloading my quiver of virtual arrows. "I don't exist anymore."

"Did you stick your head out an airlock without a helmet? You've been acting very weird."

So I tell him about the DNA results, and that quiets him down.

"But that's crazy," he says. "Of course you exist."

"Do I?" I ask, only half kidding. "How do we know?"

"I could kick you in the shin. If you say *ow*, we know you're real."

"Okay, let's assume you did that, and I passed the test. Why would all records of my family be gone?"

He shakes his head. "I don't know, but tell my dad and maybe he'll have an idea."

"He's been through enough these last few days, and he's busy trying to find the boxes."

Will shakes his head again. "No, he got back in the middle of the night. He found them! They're in quarantine!"

I turn off the game. "Quarantine?"

Will nods. "Apparently no one can get into the boxes, so they had to put them there in case they contain an unknown substance that could be dangerous. But that's not all! The commander said you couldn't have the boxes anyway. They don't become yours until you're seventeen."

"Why? And how does *he* know that?"

Will shakes his head. "That's what he told my dad, who's

at work now, by the way. He's trying to make sure he doesn't get fired and shipped off to Earth." He gives a little shudder. "Probably better if we wait till his shift is over to ask about it, okay?"

"Don't worry," I assure him. "I'm not going to bother him. I'm going straight to the source." Then I storm out of the arcade, which has started to fill up with early-morning patrons. I'm tired of people knowing things about my life that I don't.

I've never been inside the quarantine room, which is all the way at the bottom of the spaceport. I have to pass by waste disposal on my way and make sure not to make eye contact with anyone through the window. I have a feeling after today they're going to be my new best friends.

KEEP OUT is emblazoned over the quarantine room in big letters, which normally I would ignore, but something about the skull and crossbones painted on the door gives me pause.

I've heard stories about the shipments that have wound up in this room over the years. Things that slither, things that make fire, things that give off noxious odors. Those are sent right back off the station. The items that are questionable, have been mislabeled, or have no label at all are subjected to various tests. I'd really like to see what they're doing to my boxes.

I knock. No answer. Well, no one can say I didn't try. So I push open the door and let myself in. To my surprise, no one is in there. The lights are on, though, and I can see three different stations set up around the room. The Locksley boxes have been evenly divided among them. One table holds a tub of water, another an X-ray scanner, another has jars of fluid that say *Poison, Do Not Ingest* on them. The whole thing is creepy, and I don't like being here. Perhaps I do need Uncle Kent to help me.

I start to back out of the room. I've almost reached the door when that most dreaded of contacts happens — the firm grip on the shoulder by a large, strong hand.

"Hello, Robin," the commander says. "When your teacher reported you absent I figured I would find you here. Your uncle told me what happened with your parents, and I see you've found your boxes. Are you doing okay?"

Like I said, the commander is a pretty decent guy. I'm about to say something like *Robin of Locksley is always okay*, but instead I shake my head. "I'm pretty confused, actually. Maybe you can tell me why my boxes are being drowned and x-rayed and poisoned?"

He removes his hand from my shoulder. "Yeah, sorry about all this. But the packages didn't come with the necessary paperwork. We have no idea of their origins. Allowing them to be opened without testing them would be irresponsible. Do you understand?"

"I guess." I glance at the closest stack. "They're all still locked, though?"

He nods. "They all require the same combination."

"What is it?" I ask.

"We have no idea," he admits. "Our assumption is that when you turn seventeen you will receive the code somehow."

"Yeah, about that. Why do I have to be seventeen?"

To my surprise, he replies with "That's what your uncle told me. Your parents apparently gave him that instruction."

"Oh. So you haven't gotten into any of them?"

He shakes his head. "No. Now let's get you to class. I promise we'll take good care of your belongings. And if everything is deemed safe, they will be returned to you. And if one of the locks happens to be loose and you happen to peek inside, well, I never saw anything."

I give him a half smile, which is half a smile more than I'd been able to pull off since yesterday afternoon.

As the commander walks with me (or should I say, *escorts me*) back down the hall, I gather up the nerve to tell him about what Robo-teach's experiment pulled up for me. I figure he'll hear about it sooner or later, so it may as well be from me.

"What do you think it means?" I ask when I'm through.

His expression grows very serious. "I think it means that whoever erased the records of your family is trying to protect themselves. I think you should let them. Just put it all behind you and let it go."

I nod, because I know that's what he wants me to do. And because I think he's right. My parents probably paid someone to wipe out the records of their lives after their deaths, not even thinking about how it might affect me. But they left in the first place without thinking of me, either, so why am I surprised?

"Stay here and collect yourself for a minute," the commander tells me. "Then get up to school, okay?"

I nod. He starts to pat me on the shoulder when his watch buzzes and flashes red. "Commander here," he says, then hurries off on official business and leaves me alone in the hallway. I take a few breaths, look around, and dart right back into quarantine. Like he said, I'll put it all behind me — right after I get a look inside one of these boxes! I snatch the closest one — a medium-size box that was waiting to be submerged in water. I stick it under my arm and dash back out. It doesn't matter that I can't open it. Just having it makes me feel a little more in control.

When I get up to the Central Plaza, I'm surprised to see it's full of people. Last-minute dance party, maybe? But I don't see the band. Led by Robo-teach, my classmates come filing into the large open area, all talking excitedly. Will and Malaya pull up the rear. I guess doing the DNA project together has brought them closer. I think they may even be holding hands, but there are too many people in the way to tell for sure. Kind of gross, if you ask me. Sounds sweaty.

I'm still trying to process why this place is suddenly so crowded when I realize people are all pointing and staring out the observation deck over my shoulder. I quickly turn and then inhale sharply. When I passed by here not that long ago, the only thing outside was the usual boring outer space, with its stars and planets too distant to see clearly. Now an enormous white object fills the entire view. It's long and narrow and doesn't look like any airship I've ever seen. Instinctively, I step back, like that's going to do me any good if that thing plows into us.

Toby and Elan run over to me. "Do you see it, Robin?" Elan shouts even though I'm standing a foot away from him and my head is tilted back. He shouts again, "It's HUGE!"

It really *is* huge. "What is it?" I ask.

Finley joins us, and Toby and Elan wait for him to explain. As annoying as he is, being the commander's son means he can usually be counted on to know the latest news.

Finley meets my eyes and then glances away. Guess he's still afraid I'll gossip about his family's less-than-stellar past.

But his excitement over whatever that thing is outside overpowers his usual habit of insulting or ignoring me. "A passenger airship from Earth has sent a distress signal!" he declares. "They need to dock here, but they're too big to approach nose-first like the regular ships."

Elan jumps in with a whole explanation about torque and gravitational spin and other science-y things I don't understand. All I know is that the giant ship has to match our orbit and then twist around until the grabbers can reach its mid-deck. Or something like that.

"What've you got there?" Toby suddenly asks. He's pointing at the box under my arm. I'd actually forgotten I was carrying it! I try to twist my arm behind me, but it doesn't matter. They're all gathering around to get a closer look.

"It's not important right now," I insist, shoving it under a bench. "I'll show you later." I have no intention of showing any of them later.

The commander's voice fills the air, and everyone's attention thankfully turns toward the bridge of the command deck above our heads.

"As everyone can see, we have unexpected guests. Their ship is in need of repairs, but it isn't expected to take long. A day or two at most. Still, I expect everyone to make the passengers feel at home."

This announcement sets everyone chattering again. We've never, at least in my memory, had "guests" here. Any passenger ships would go to another spaceport — *any* other one. This ship must really be in a bad way or else there's no way they'd choose us.

So basically no one wants to leave the plaza because we all want to see what's about to happen. Even though I'm anxious to see if I can break into the box, I'm more curious about this ship. After another hour of the ship inching toward us, and a lot of banging and clanging, the commander announces that we've been able to connect to their mid-ship emergency escape hatch. A cheer rises from the crowd and we all stream out of the plaza to wait outside Shane's garage, which is where they will be arriving.

I don't know what kind of guests I'm expecting, but everyone around me is speculating that they must be super rich, or royalty even, if they're flying in something like that. Some think it might even be Prince John himself. Even though we up here aren't affiliated with any particular planet, being so close (relatively) to Earth, we're aware of their political leaders. I've never seen a prince before, so that'd be pretty cool.

But when the passengers file down the entry platform, there doesn't appear to be a prince among them, at least no one in a crown and flowing robes, which is how I picture a prince would look. Instead there's an old guy in a wheelchair pushed by a tall, younger guy, followed by three kids around my age. They're all wearing variations of white clothes (pure white, not at all green). One of the boys and one of the girls has brown skin, and the other boy's skin is fair, but with more red to it than ours, the mark of a life lived where the sun shines. They all look a bit shell-shocked, carrying bags and suitcases. Wherever they were headed to in their fancy ship, I can't blame them for being disappointed to wind up here.

A hoverbuggy whisks the two men away toward the medi-station. As the crowd parts to let them through, I catch sight of one last girl heading down the platform. She walks with more confidence than the rest, with her shoulders back and her head held high. She's carrying two suitcases, one large, one small. Her gaze sweeps across the crowd, almost like she's looking for someone. Without knowing why, I push through a few rows of people until I'm right up front. When her sharp blue eyes meet mine, a jolt runs through my body.

I've just met my person.

CHAPTER EIGHT

Marian

Everything feels like it's moving in slow motion. Or maybe it's just me that's out of sync, standing here in front of dozens of strangers, doing my best to pretend I have a pillow on my head like I was taught in etiquette class. I focus on keeping my gaze soft and steady and my expression pleasant, just as if I were being led into one of my parents' fancy events. Inside, though, I'm shaking like a leaf.

Just an hour ago I was standing at the wall of the airship with my heart ready to leap out of my chest at the sheer jaw-dropping beauty of space. If I thought the glittering lights of The City were numerous, they were a spoonful of what we were speeding through. Only seeing my own face reflected in the glass surface with the image of outer space behind it made me accept this wasn't a dream. I could have stood there forever if PJ's voice hadn't come over the speakers announcing we were making a pit stop to refuel.

Asher pulled himself away from the view to ask, "Why would we need to refuel already? We just left Earth a few hours ago. I mean, I know we're traveling super fast, but still."

The rest of us just shrugged. To be honest, I couldn't really focus on something as mundane and ordinary as fuel. An entire universe that had previously been invisible to me was revealing itself with a show more spectacular than I could ever have imagined. I still knew it had been a mistake that I was selected for this journey, but I was now beyond grateful for the error.

Our acceleration slowed to a crawl a few minutes later and the lights dimmed. That was the first time I felt a flicker of concern. Instead of stars zooming past us, huge chunks of what looked like ice drifted by. They were far enough away not to cross our path, but it was still a bit unnerving. Then a huge round structure encircled with flashing lights appeared right in front of us. As we stared, two parallel red beams shot out into space, forming an odd kind of runway. Our ship made a half turn and adjusted course until we were lined right up with it.

Asher declared that the station we were floating toward was called Delta Z, and began rattling off details about the history of spaceports and how Delta Z is a particularly old one. "No passenger ship from Earth has docked there for over a hundred years," he recited, like he was delivering a report to our teacher. "Not with much more modern facilities only a few light-years away."

"We're not in school anymore, Asher," Sarena told him. "You don't have to try to impress us with your knowledge and your big words."

Asher swept a chunk of his blond hair out of his eyes. "That's true," he said, smiling with one side of his mouth. "I only need to impress *you*."

"You wish!" Sarena shot back, rolling her eyes. But the corners of her mouth twitched up.

PJ ran into the room, barely glancing at us as he checked data on the tablet he was holding. "We'll be hooking on in five minutes," he announced. "I'll need all of you to grab your suitcases and be ready to disembark."

"Our suitcases?" Asher asked. "Why would we need our suitcases for a fuel stop? And why do we need to refuel already, anyway? If we burn up fuel at this rate, we won't reach Earth Beta for months."

I finally started to pay attention. PJ hesitated, and I noticed his eyes were red, almost like he had been crying. I stepped forward and put my hand on his arm without thinking. Then I pulled it back, hiding my hand under my sleeve. People of my social status did not reach out and touch others, especially those we don't know well. My cheeks began to burn. Sarena stepped in and asked him, "Are you all right, PJ?"

He shook his head. "We have a small crack in one of the fuel lines. We're in no danger at this point, but the captain felt it would be best to repair it now, before we leave the sun's orbit completely. At that point the autopilot will navigate to Earth Beta and it's much more complicated to stop."

"And?" Sarena prompts. "That's not all, is it?"

He shook his head again. "It's my grandfather. He tried to help by crawling into one of the maintenance tubes and got an electric shock. He's . . . he's not doing well. I need to take him to the medical station immediately when we dock."

The expressions on all of our faces must have shown our confusion. Gareth spoke up first. "What do you mean? Wouldn't his medi-bots mend any injuries?"

"The medi-bots are linked to the life support systems on Earth," PJ said wearily. "They don't work in space." Now our surprise turned to alarm. "Don't worry," he quickly added. "They'll be up and running again as soon as we get to Earth Beta." He gave a small chuckle. "Try not to fall down any stairs till then."

None of us laughed back.

PJ grew serious again. "I'm going back up to the control center to be with him. When you step onto that spaceport you'll need to be on your best behavior; you're representing our planet." His eyes swept over us, lingering on Gareth. "As soon as we get to Earth Beta, you're getting a haircut."

Gareth's hand immediately went out to grab his ponytail. He may have emitted a little whimper.

It's now six minutes later, and I'm standing in a spaceport. I've heard of them, of course, but never thought about what it might be like to go to one. In my head, I'd pictured them looking like our buildings on Earth, or like the building-shaped airship that brought us here. But it's nothing like that at all. It's round, for starters, and made of materials that I've never seen before. And the clothes! They are simple and utilitarian, and they are *all green*!

The crowd smiles at us as we enter, and a few of the younger kids wave their arms in greeting. It's obvious from their wide, expectant expressions that they're as curious about us as we are about them. How strange it must be to live up here.

My eyes land on a boy around my age, maybe a little older. He has nearly black hair and the greenest eyes I've ever seen. They seem to be boring a hole straight through mine. The color reminds me of the jewel in the headpiece Grandmother gave me. I'm now very glad she made me take it. It's a little piece of her so very far away from home.

I can't pull my gaze away from his for what feels like a really long time. Long enough for Sarena to make a little "ahem" sound and nudge me. I force myself to turn my attention toward the man in uniform striding toward us.

Seeing how the crowd parts for him, he's clearly the captain of the station.

"Welcome, visitors, to Spaceport Delta Z." He spreads his arms wide. "She isn't much to look at, but we're mighty proud of her. I'm Commander Harlon. Please make yourselves at home while your ship is being repaired. We have the finest mechanics this side of the Milky Way. And don't worry about your teacher — he's in good hands with our nurse. She'll fix him right up."

"Let me guess," Asher says. "She's the finest nurse this side of the Milky Way?"

The residents laugh, and the commander grins. "As a matter of fact, she is." From anyone else, Asher's comment would have come out sounding obnoxious. I steal a glance at the black-haired boy in time to see him roll his eyes. Guess Asher's charm doesn't work on other teenage boys. Or at least, not this one. I stifle a laugh.

The commander gestures for one of the older boys to join him. "This is my son, Finley. He'll take you all to the arcade to relax with some old-timey video games. Collecting them is a hobby of mine."

He beams, clearly proud of this. I'm not entirely sure what a hobby is, or what an old-timey video game would even look like, but I feel a stir of curiosity. It's different than the awe I feel at being here in this foreign place, as the stars stream around us. The curiosity comes from that part of my brain that is hungry all the time, and I don't mean for vita-squares.

"Let's go," Finley says, waving for us to follow him. His voice is not yet as commanding as his father's, but it will be soon.

The green-eyed boy suddenly rushes toward me and lunges for my big suitcase! I instinctively pull back, stepping on Sarena's toes in the process.

"So sorry!" I gasp as she lets out a small yelp.

"You look like you could use some help," the boy tells me, reaching for the handle again.

I jerk back farther the second time, knocking into Sarena again and apologizing as she rubs her upper arm this time. I'm not entirely sure why I'm reacting this way. The suitcase really *is* big, thanks to that abandoner Ivy, who insisted I should be prepared for any situation. Bet she hadn't been programmed to consider *this* one! And it's true that I have little experience (okay, none) lugging heavy objects, but Grandmother's headpiece is packed in there, and I will never forgive myself if it went missing. Gareth offering to carry it to my room on the airship was different. I simply cannot entrust this treasure to a stranger. And he is *definitely* strange, with his green clothes and eyes like emeralds and black hair so deep it almost looks purple.

"I'm fine," I snap.

The boy doesn't reply, only tilts his head up at me. Then he seems to find his voice. "The arcade is on the other end of the spaceport, and I'm stronger than I look. Stronger than you, certainly." He grins a bright, wide smile that's lost on me.

"How do you know how strong or weak I am?" I tighten my hold on the suitcase. A boy a little younger than him is trying to get his attention by pulling on his shirt, but he's ignoring him. In my ear, Sarena hisses, "Let him take it! He's flirting with you."

My eyes widen at that. Insulting me is his way of saying

he likes me? Maybe that's how it works and I'm simply clueless. I have no experience meeting a new boy my own age. I've known all the others on my rung of society's ladder my whole life. I'm certain this boy would not be a suitable match, so why bother?

Sarena hisses at me again. "For goodness sake, Marian, you don't need to *marry him*, just give him your suitcase so we can all move on!"

CHAPTER NINE

↞ Robin ↠

"Cousin, you've got *no* game!" Will says, shaking his head at me as we join the large group now headed toward the arcade. I fold my arms over my chest and scowl. Both my arms are free to fold because *I'm* not the one carrying the pretty girl's suitcase, *Will* is. Apparently she deemed him the safer bet just because he didn't lunge at her like her suitcase was the last vita-square in the galaxy.

"I've got plenty of game," I argue. Although admittedly today's events are making me question my skills. I can usually charm anyone into anything. A compliment about the lunch lady's hairstyle always ensures an extra square is tossed my way. At dinner Uncle Kent no longer asks me to clean the dishes, not after I "accidentally" dropped them so many times. Even the commander doesn't yell at me for riding my hoverboard in restricted travel lanes because I can always tell him what playing card he's holding and he loves magic tricks.

But the truth of it is, I've never spoken to a girl my own age who I felt this way about, let alone one with flowing hair the color of the corn in our birthday meals. And her eyes! Blue like the sky in the image of my ancestor in the photo that has now disappeared without a trace. And she's smart! It shone through when she looked at me. I know that sounds sappy, but it's the truth.

But the coolest thing about the girl is her voice. She's said only twelve words to me, but they came out like notes of a song. An angry song, sure, but one I can still hear playing in my head. When I first heard her talk it rendered me unable to speak and I probably looked like a dork, just staring at her mutely.

Okay, clearly I'm in trouble.

"Maybe you're right," I grumble to Will out of the corner of my mouth. The last thing I need is for the girl to hear me. She's sticking very close to her suitcase, only turning away briefly to gawk at the observation deck as we pass by it. "Tell me what I'm supposed to do," I whisper. "How do I get her to like me?"

He glances over at me. "How many days since you've changed into fresh clothes?"

I follow his gaze. My shirt is stained, a hole has popped up over one knee, and a string dangles from the hem of my sleeve. I don't reply.

"Go to our home unit and change your clothes. Maybe wash your face and comb your hair, too. Girls like a boy who looks put together."

I stare at him. "Where do you get this stuff?"

He rolls his eyes. "It's common sense."

"Fine." I sigh. "I'll meet you at the arcade."

It only takes me five minutes to get to our home unit, which is one of the closest ones to the Central Plaza. One of the perks of being here so long.

I scramble through my drawers, pulling out, then discarding, shirt after shirt until I find one that only has a slight stain. If I wear it backward, she shouldn't even notice it. The pants are more difficult. I never considered how shabby my wardrobe had become.

I wind up taking a pair of Will's pants instead. He's a little shorter than me, so I push down the waistband a few inches and tighten my belt so my ankles won't peek out. I run the risk of them falling down on me, but at least they're clean and in one piece.

Just before I leave Will's room I spot the hat he sewed in class the other day. He did a good job on it, much better than I did. I didn't even finish mine. I plop the hat on my head and turn from side to side, admiring it in the mirror over his dresser. I look very dapper! I've heard Uncle Kent use that word to describe one of the pilots who stayed on the station for a few days last month while his ship was in for routine maintenance. He'd worn a suit and hat the whole time and used to tilt his hat at people as they passed by. Now that I think of it, he dined with a different woman each meal! Maybe Will knows what he's talking about after all.

I need one last thing to complete the look.

"You've got to be kidding me," Will says when I show up at the arcade a few minutes later. I hop off my hoverboard, swing it under my arm, and beam at him.

"How great do I look?"

He opens his mouth, then closes it again. Then he sighs. "Actually, you look pretty great. No one but you could carry that off."

I'm suddenly flanked by all four of the kids from the airship. "Is that . . . is that a real feather in your hat?" the boy with the long, dark hair asks. "From a real . . . animal?"

I nod proudly. "It's from a bird. A macaw, we think."

"Can I touch it?" he asks.

"Sure, have at it." I tilt my head toward him, and he reaches up and runs his hand over the feather.

"So soft!" he exclaims.

The others reach out now, all except the girl with the yellow hair who I'm trying to impress. She's hanging back, looking at me out of the corners of her eyes. Will nudges me from behind and I step closer to the girl. Only a little, though. No pouncing this time. I may not be the sharpest tack in the toolbox when it comes to romance, but I'm a quick learner.

I reach up and pull the feather out of my hat. "Would you like to see it?"

She hesitates, then nods. She takes it reverently, like she's afraid it will break. For something that looks so fragile, it's held up perfectly so far. "Where did you get a real feather?" she asks in that lyrical voice of hers. It takes a few seconds to recover from hearing it again.

"It's a very long story," I tell her. "Maybe we can take a walk and I could tell you?"

The girl shakes her head and thrusts the feather back at me. "I couldn't. I don't know you."

"Too forward," Will hisses in my ear. He's right, of course.

"I understand," I tell her in my most polite and respectful voice. I don't have much practice using it, though, so my words come out sounding more sarcastic than I intended. I clear my throat and wave my hand around the room. "We can get to know each other while we play a game, then. Any one you'd like."

Her eyes scan the large room and land on BullsEye. "That one," she says, and heads toward it.

Perfect. I'm fairly certain impressing a girl with your mad archery skills is a step in the right direction. I leave Will guarding her two suitcases and hurry after. She's already standing in position, her arm pulled back to release a virtual arrow. All my classmates and her three travel mates have gathered to watch.

"Good luck," I tell her as I drop a token into the machine.

Her first three shots land an inch away from the bull's-eye. The last one makes it to within half an inch. Everyone around us cheers. Her score is good enough to put her on the high score board — far below mine and Will's, of course.

That is how I learn her name is Marian.

"Your turn," Marian says, stepping aside. My classmates (well, most of them) begin chanting my name. "Robin! Robin!" They know how good I am at this game.

Just as I'm about to let loose my first arrow, I glance over my shoulder and catch Will's eye. He shakes his head at me. I frown. What's he trying to tell me? He gives another small shake and mimics letting an arrow fly into the corner of the room. He wants me to throw the game and let her win! It goes against all my instincts, but I guess his coaching has gotten me this far. I send my first arrow far off the mark.

"It's okay," Marian says encouragingly. "Just hold your elbow a little higher."

So now she's coaching me like this is my first time. I grit my teeth. Will better be right! My second arrow is a little closer, but still really far. When the next two don't even land on the screen, the boys in my class shake their heads in disgust. The girls are looking at me with something bordering on respect. I only care about the opinion of one girl right now, though. And she's holding her hand over her mouth like she's about to be sick! Oh, wait. She's trying to keep herself from laughing at me.

"It's not nice to make fun of people, you know," I tease her. "Not all of us are as good as you."

She lowers her hand and does her best to maintain a straight face. "Beginner's luck," she claims.

I doubt that, but I let it go. I couldn't be more surprised when she boldly steps over to me, links her arm through mine, and says, "Okay, we can go for a walk now. Anyone willing to lose that spectacularly must be a good guy." Her three friends quickly surround us.

My cheeks redden. I've been called many things (most of them not complimentary), but no one has called me a good guy before. I'll need to reveal another magic trick to that savvy cousin of mine.

"You can show me the observation deck that we passed before," she says. Then to her friends she adds, "I'll be fine. Don't look so worried."

"I'll take your belongings to your room," the long-haired boy says.

"Thank you, Gareth."

The other girl gives Marian's arm a squeeze, and we're off. I point out different parts of the station as we pass, aware that I'm babbling a little, but I'm afraid if an awkward silence descends on us that I'll say something much more stupid. I get quite a few raised eyebrows as we cross the station (and a thumbs-up from Shane when I point out the garage), but no one stops us.

I lead her onto the same bench I'd sat on with Uncle Kent and Will just a few days ago. "So how'd you know that I threw the game?"

"I saw the name Robin at the top of the high score board," she admits. "When your friends started chanting that name I put it together."

"Ah, clever. Hadn't thought of that."

She looks out at the stars, then back into the station, then shakes her head.

"What?" I ask.

"It's just so strange that people live here on this round ball, floating in space in the middle of nowhere."

I laugh. "Doesn't that describe where you live, too?"

Her lips turn up. I get the impression she doesn't smile nearly often enough. "You're right," she says. "I never thought of it that way."

We talk for a long time about her life on Earth and what her family is like. I can tell by the way she winces that she was hurt by how quickly they sent her away. I tell her about my hobbies, and she seems genuinely surprised and says she has no time to pursue any of her own interests. "I wouldn't even know what they were," she admits.

Some of life on Earth is similar to Delta Z — the lack of colors and no real food source — but most things are not. Life down there sounds both incredible (hovercars! skyscrapers! sunshine! medi-bots!) and awful (nano-trackers, the blackened wastelands, the fact that they only have five hundred more years until their oxygen runs out).

"I had never seen the stars before this morning," she says, waving her hand around at the scene surrounding us. "Now I never want to stop seeing them."

Honestly, the swirling stars still just make me dizzy, but I don't mention that. "Tell me about the sun."

She pauses for a few seconds, then says, "Well, it makes you hot and sweaty if it's summertime. Provides light when it's daytime. It used to make things grow, but that was before. Now the sunsets are the best part. That's when the sky fills with colors that you could swim in, not that I have ever been swimming in anything. I used to watch them with my grandmother whenever I didn't have something scheduled." She clasps her hands in her lap. "I guess that doesn't tell you much."

"It does," I tell her. "It tells me a lot."

She looks up and smiles at me then, a real one. She's getting better at it. My heart speeds up.

"How'd you get to be so good at the archery game?" I ask. "I'm not buying the beginner's luck thing."

She looks out into space again, but I don't think she sees the stars this time. "My father and I used to play it together for hours when I was younger. I guess I got pretty good at it." Her voice hardens when she talks about her father. I'll have to remember that. Speaking of fathers . . . I reach down and feel around under the bench.

"Phew," I say out loud as I slide out the box I'd stashed earlier. "It's still here." Apparently meeting a girl can make one forget even the most important things!

Marian leans forward. "What is that?"

"It's a long story."

"You seem to have a lot of those."

I balance the box on my lap and rest my hands on top. "My parents sent it to me. At least, I think they did. They're gone now. They've been gone a long time, really." It feels strange saying those words out loud, but not strange saying them to her.

"I'm sorry to hear that," she says. "What's inside?"

"No idea." I show her the locks. "I don't have the code." I don't mention that I'm not supposed to open it until I'm seventeen.

"How about using your digi-pen?" she asks. "You have those up here, right?"

“Yes, but how would the digi-pen do something like that? They’re only for storing data. And writing, I mean.”

Her eyes widen. “You can *write* with yours?”

I nod. “Not that there’s much to write on — no paper or anything, of course. You can’t?”

She shakes her head. “All communications have to go through the interwebs. Nothing is private.” She’s lost in thought for a minute, but then perks up. “Mine can do other things, though.” She reaches into a pocket on the side of her dress and pulls out a digi-pen that looks almost exactly like mine.

“This one is empty of data,” she explains, turning it over in her hand. “My old one is . . . well . . . I had to leave it on Earth.” She scrolls through some settings and then holds up the tip of the pen. It’s glowing white-hot!

“Mine *definitely* doesn’t do that!” I exclaim. Shane has some tools at the garage that heat up, but I hadn’t thought of using them to melt the lock. It’s a brilliant idea. “Can you show me how to use it?”

Marian adjusts the temperature setting until I can actually see waves of heat rising from the tip of the pen. Careful to face it away from us, she holds the pen up to the box and traces a circle around the lock. Whatever material the box is made of sizzles. A few seconds later the lock falls off, right into my hand.

We lock eyes and beam at each other. I throw open the lid, and we bend our heads to look inside.

Well. I certainly didn’t expect *that*!

CHAPTER TEN

Marian

Sitting on a bench in the middle of outer space and talking to a boy I only met this morning is already strange enough. Doing it while draped in three shimmering gold chains is a whole other level of bizarre. No gold has existed in Earth's crust for hundreds of years, nor on any other planet known to us. This is a treasure beyond measure.

Robin hasn't spoken in the last ten minutes. I'm not even certain he has blinked. He just keeps staring back and forth between the necklaces, the now-empty box, and the data chip in his palm. I'm pretty sure he's in shock, and I can't say I blame him. I reluctantly return the chains to him before anyone else comes into the observation deck. He stuffs them in his pockets.

Before opening the box, he was much easier to talk to than I would have expected due to my utter lack of experience. I suppose all those etiquette classes on "how to make conversation in various social situations" have paid off. I should probably see if I can help him recover his wits.

I move my hand toward him, pull it back, then reach forward again until my fingertips are gently resting on his forearm. "Um, Robin? Do you want me to use my digi-pen to read the chip? Maybe it's a letter explaining this. Or maybe you want to do it alone, in private? I'd understand. You hardly know me."

Wordlessly, he hands me the tiny chip. I guess I proved my trustworthiness by not running off with the gold. Not that there's anywhere to run in a spaceport!

I slide the chip into the slot on the side of the pen, and face the tip away from us. Instantly a holo-screen appears, filling with words and images of items I've only seen in classroom videos of the past. Much of it I've never seen before at all. More jewelry, cups, bowls, clothing, a folding chair, drawings, coins, a pocket-sized golden statue of a large-bellied man, two swords, a dagger, a pair of sky-blue elbow-length gloves, clear and brown glass bottles labeled *OINTMENT* and *CREAM*, and on and on.

"It's an inventory," I say, stating the obvious. I point to the left side of the screen. "I think it's telling us what objects are in each box."

He nods in agreement, but he still isn't speaking. I turn off the pen and the screen disappears with it. Then Robin is on his feet, his words tumbling out.

"What am I supposed to do with this? First, my parents totally disappear from my life, then they — or possibly someone else — sends me all this after they die? How did they possibly get all this stuff? What good does it do me? How am I supposed to feel?" He throws up his arms and takes a breath. Then he sits back down. "Sorry. Got a little carried away there."

"It's a lot to process," I assure him. "What *are* you going to do with it all?"

He stares down at the box, then shakes his head. "I have no idea. I could sell or barter it, I guess, but there's nothing I need up here that I don't already have. How about I just don't think about it? That's worked for me in the past."

"Me, too," I admit. "Although it catches up with you

sooner or later. At least you know your parents were thinking of you, right? I mean, better late than never?"

"I guess so. I'll never get a chance to thank them, though." He runs his fingers through his hair, knocking his hat to the floor. "Ugh, forgot I was still wearing that."

I pick up the hat and place it back on his head, adjusting the feather so it sticks out at an angle. "It suits you."

He smiles gratefully. I smile back. We sit there like that and I wait for it to feel awkward, but it doesn't. Finally, I clear my throat. "Now that you've shared this treasure with me, I feel like it's only fair if I show you something. It isn't made of gold, but it's a treasure, nonetheless."

"You don't have to," he says. "Not if it's something you want to keep private."

"I want to."

He stands up and waits for me to join him. When I remain seated, he says, "Isn't it in your suitcase? You seemed very attached to that."

I shake my head and reach for my boot. I wiggle my finger down far enough until I feel the folded piece of paper, then slide it out and hand it to Robin.

"What is this?" he asks, rubbing it between his fingers. "I've never felt anything exactly like it before."

"It's paper," I whisper. "Real paper."

His eyes widen. Slowly, he unfolds it and spreads it out on his palm. "What do these letters and numbers mean? It looks like some sort of code."

I hadn't planned what to say about it; I'd just wanted to show him. But of course he'd want to know. "I think — but don't know for sure — that if we can figure out the code it will tell us what happened to King Richard."

His eyes widen again. "King Richard? Didn't he leave Earth years ago on some kind of mission?"

"That's what everyone thinks. But he may never have left at all." I do my best to recite the confusing conversation I'd overheard. I tell him I stole the code after scanning it into my old digi-pen and writing a fake one in the notebook. I run my finger over the middle of my palm. If that accident happened now, without the medi-bots, I'd have a painful blister. What a strange thought.

Robin tilts his head at me, his eyes twinkling. "Well, well, Marian. Aren't you the little sneak? It seems there's more to you than just a pretty face."

I punch him on the arm and he laughs. Okay, so it was my first punch and he probably barely felt it.

"Have you tried to decipher it yet?" he asks.

I shake my head. "I hadn't even thought of that."

"Isn't that why you took it?" he asks.

I realize this is a reasonable question, but I shrug. "I just wanted the paper." It sounds lame, even to my ears. I wait for him to express some kind of disappointment that I hadn't tried to help somehow, but Robin only says, "I don't blame you. You don't want to mess with Prince John. He's not a good guy from what we hear up here. Why get involved with other people's troubles?"

So now I'm the one left with the vague sense of disappointment.

"Sorry to interrupt you beating up my cousin," a voice says from behind us. It's the boy who introduced himself earlier as Will. "I punch him a lot, too." He turns to Robin. "You should have seen their airship! That kid Asher who likes to hear himself talk gave us a tour. It was unreal! There were fifteen floors and —" He breaks off when he sees the paper in Robin's hand. "What is that?"

Robin glances at me, and I nod permission. Will snatches the paper and I wince, but it doesn't rip.

"It's a code," I tell him. "Before you ask, I have no idea how to break it. I couldn't, even if I wanted to. We are not taught those kinds of skills where I'm from."

"We are," Will says. "But you don't need code-breaking skills to read this. It's not a code."

"What do you mean?" I ask, taking the paper from him and looking harder at what's written there.

"These are coordinates," Will says. "Sometimes the pilots let me and Robin hang around in their cockpits when they come to the station." He points down at each line as he speaks. "It pinpoints a place relative to the celestial equator. This number shows you the right ascension, this is the declination, and the third number marks the distance from the sun, or the horizon center — I'm not certain which one."

"So what you're saying is that I could use this to find someone back on Earth?"

He nods. "The pilot would put these coordinates into the ship's navigation system, and they would take you right to him or her. Who's missing? Does this have something to do with Robin's parents?"

Robin stands up. "No, of course not. Thanks for actually paying attention when we went on those ships. I was always distracted by the knobs and levers and shiny bits. Forget Elan — I'm going to have to start cheating off *you* in class!"

Will looks disappointed, but Robin is right to keep the truth from him. And he was right about Prince John. He *is* dangerous, and I can't risk anyone else getting involved.

I have a lot to figure out, starting with how I'm going to convince PJ to turn the airship around without telling him why.

King Richard was my friend. And I need to help him. I wouldn't have thought I needed to go into outer space to figure that out.

CHAPTER ELEVEN

↞ Robin ↠

"Never going to happen," PJ tells us when we find him in the back of Shane's garage. When the nurse told Marian and me that Captain Pratchett was sleeping soundly, this was the next place I suggested we look for PJ. Sooner or later, every visitor finds his way back here. Usually sooner.

"But it wouldn't take hardly any time at all," Marian argues. "You could drop me off and be back here in less than a day."

PJ shakes his head. "It doesn't work like that. I could explain about escape velocities and hyperbolic orbits and the fact that we are on autopilot to Earth Beta, but that would be the long way of simply saying no. So . . . no. Sorry, kid."

Marian's shoulders sag. PJ steps toward the card table, sees the buy-in amount, and backs away to watch the game instead. I glance over at Shane, who must have just come from working on the *Royal Horizon*, a few feet of rubber tubing slung over his shoulder. He tosses it in the recycling pile and then catches my eye. I raise my eyebrow toward PJ, and Shane gives me a nearly imperceptible nod in reply. This is where Shane shines. He approaches PJ and casually puts his arm around his shoulder.

"PJ, good buddy who I only met five minutes ago . . . it's your first time here, so how about you join in for free?"

PJ doesn't protest. They never do. He grabs a seat. "Deal me in!"

Fifteen minutes later, when he loses (they almost always lose) and can't pay, Shane works his magic. "That'll be six hundred quid."

PJ's eyes widen. "But I don't have that."

Shane shrugs. "What've you got, then?"

"I can, um, show you around the ship? Give you the private tour?"

"Nah," Shane says. "Seen a lot of airships."

PJ fumbles in his pockets but comes up empty.

"How about this?" Shane proposes. "How about you drop this young lady back off on Earth before going on your way? We'll call it even."

"I truly can't," PJ insists. "It's just not possible."

I glance at Marian. She's watching the whole exchange with a mixture of horror and concern. Shane's methods aren't exactly on the up-and-up, but this is how he gets half of the stuff he owns. I think he even won his beat-up old shuttlecraft this way. That poor sap must have owed a ton of money.

"What if instead of taking Marian home," I suggest, "you let her stay here with us until a ship can take her back to Earth?"

PJ considers this for a minute, then asks, "But what would I tell the folks on Earth Beta who are expecting her?"

That's a tricky one. To my surprise, Marian speaks up. "Tell them I caught a cold on Delta Z and you didn't want to risk spreading it."

Shane looks impressed, and I admit, I am, too. It's a brilliant solution. PJ sighs. "This must be very important to you."

"It is," Marian says.

"You'll be giving up the opportunity of a lifetime to visit another planet."

She nods. "I know. But at least I got here, right?" She glances at me, and I feel a warmth spread through my chest. I'm a goner with this one.

PJ stabs his finger at Shane and me. "You are both responsible for her from this moment on. If I hear you harmed one hair on her head, this little gambling ring you've got going on will come crashing down. And that's just for starters."

"You can count on us," Shane says. "Right, Robin?"

"You bet," I reply.

"My betting days might be over," PJ mutters. "Now scram before I change my mind."

"Just one more thing, PJ," Marian says. "Please don't tell anyone at school. Or my parents. They'll see me soon enough, so I don't want them to worry."

"I'll give you two days," he says. "Once we get to Earth Beta, it will be out of my control."

"Thank you," Marian says. "And, PJ, I'm glad your grandfather is going to be okay."

"Me, too," he says. "Now scram."

So we scram.

"Can't say I approve of his methods," Marian says when we reach the Central Plaza. "First let them play, then make them pay? But I admit it was effective. So now what?"

"Now we find the commander and ask if any ships are heading our way with enough room for a passenger."

"Can you do that while I find my classmates? I'll need to explain why I'm not going with them. I guess I'll say I'm homesick."

"Are you?"

She pauses for a few seconds, then shakes her head. "I miss my grandmother, and my maid, Ivy, but my parents were so quick to get rid of me I think they'll be disappointed when I show up tomorrow."

"Might not be tomorrow," I tell her.

"Well, the next day, then. Either way, they were expecting three months off."

She says good night before I can explain that it might not be the next day, either. Sometimes we go weeks without getting any ships, and they could be going in any of a number of directions. Guess I should have mentioned that when I suggested the idea. Should I explain it now?

Nah. I'll see her in the morning.

I double back to Shane's. He's about to head back out to the *Horizon* when I stop him and explain the problem. "Yeah," he says, "I just figured you were trying to keep her here longer by promising another ship could take her. It's clear you're sweet on her."

"Sweet on her?" I repeat with a grimace. "Who says that anymore?"

He grins. "May be corny, doesn't mean it's not true."

I gesture behind me. "Any chance we can take the shuttlecraft? I can program in the coordinates and put it on auto. We wouldn't need a pilot."

Shane chuckles. "That old craft can barely make it around the station and back, let alone half a light-year away. The corrosion component fan and the photon stabilizer still need replacing, and the pressure clamp is — wait, did you say *we*? *We* are going? Like you and her both?"

That catches me off guard. Did I say *we*? I think I did! I grin. "Guess I'm going to Earth!" I still shudder a little, out of habit.

“Not so fast there, little buddy. Have you told your uncle?”

“I only knew myself about ten seconds ago. Plus, he’s not my real uncle, you know.”

Shane steps back and studies me. “He’s as much your uncle as the nose on your face.”

“Huh?”

“You know what I mean. That man took you in and raised you as his own.”

“Did you know all this time? About my parents? Did you also know that all records of them have been erased?”

Shane nods. “Your uncle told me about the boxes arriving, and we all saw the teacher’s report about the records. I’m sorry, Robin.” He puts his hand on my shoulder, leaving a nice grease stain behind. “They were good people doing important work. I hope you’ll always remember that.”

I stare at him, hard. “What do you mean? What important work?”

Shane holds up his hands. “Hey, I really don’t know, honest. That’s just what I remember hearing when your uncle brought you here.”

I have no reason to doubt him. And anyway, I don’t want to be mad at Shane, I don’t even want to be mad at my parents. After all, I never even thought to miss them until they were gone. I’ve had a great life on Delta Z. They must have had very important reasons to go, and someone must have had an equally important reason for wiping out the trail they left behind, including the part of their trail that is *me*. And that’s only in some database; the real me is just fine.

I take a deep breath and smile at my old friend. “Guess I’m off on my own adventure, then.”

He squeezes my shoulder again, then lets go.

"Hey, I have something for you." I fish around in my pocket and pull out one of the gold chains. "This was in one of the boxes — which, yes, I know I wasn't supposed to open. But it's my way of saying thank you. For everything." He takes the chain and almost falls over in surprise. He's still speechless as I dash out.

Uncle Kent doesn't take the news as easily when I find him back at our home unit. He crosses his arms. "I know you're upset about everything with your parents, but running away isn't the answer. You're going to leave your home to go to a dying planet with a strange girl you just met? You, who — no offense — isn't known for his selflessness?"

"Um, I guess so?"

Uncle Kent begins to pace around our small living space. "I knew Delta Z wouldn't hold you forever. I just thought it would be a few more years."

"I'm coming back, Uncle Kent, don't worry."

"I've heard *that* before," he says.

"I know. But I'm not them."

"I know you're not." He gives a long, rattling sigh. "All right. Next ship in that direction. If they'll take you, that is."

I hold up one of the other gold chains and then stuff it back in my pocket. "I think they'll take us."

After he recovers from the shock and hears my explanation, he sits unmoving for quite a while. "Have you opened any of the others?"

I shake my head. "They're still in quarantine."

"We need to talk to the commander about releasing them. And you'll need his permission to leave the station on your own — not that he'd try to stop you, but there's a process." He scratches at the stubble on his chin. "Boy, you go years without much happening up here and then suddenly everything changes."

I swallow hard. "I know." Then I add, "Is it okay if I talk to the commander myself?"

He looks surprised. "You sure?"

I nod. "Plus, it's almost your shift, and I'm pretty sure Vinnie is going to beat you up if he winds up on the ceiling again."

"Guess you may as well start practicing taking care of your affairs."

I want to reassure him that I'm not going to be gone forever, but the way these last few days have gone, I'm starting to doubt my ability to predict anything anymore.

Finley is in the command center with the commander when I walk in. He startles a bit when he sees me, his eyes darting to his father and back. He doesn't need to worry; I have no plans to reveal any part of his family's history.

"I'm sorry to bother you, Commander. Can I talk to you for a minute?"

The commander presses a few buttons on his massive control screen, adjusting the lighting levels to the nighttime setting. He then turns toward me. "Ah, it's Robin. Twice in one day I get the pleasure of your company. Lucky me."

"I'll be quick," I tell him. "First, I want to give you this." I pull a strand of gold out of my pocket. "You've always treated me fairly and with kindness, and I know I didn't always deserve that."

He takes the chain and lets it dangle from his hand. Finley looks like someone who just won the intergalactic lottery.

"It was inside one of my parents' boxes," I continue. "I'm sorry I took it from quarantine and opened it, but I'm pretty sure I didn't release a deadly virus onto the spaceport. The box contained only the necklaces and an inventory of a bunch of random items from the other boxes."

Since neither of them has found their voices, I keep going. "Plus, I would like permission to ask the next ship heading to Earth if it would take me and Marian with them."

"Who's Marian?" Finley asks, still mesmerized by the swinging chain.

I feel like I've known Marian forever, but of course it's only been a few hours. "She's the yellow-haired girl from the *Royal Horizon*. She needs to go back home, and her own ship must continue its course. So do I have your permission?"

The commander clears his throat and hands the chain back to me. "I did not think you'd be able to resist opening the boxes. I'm surprised you stopped at one."

I chuckle. I should have figured him leaving me behind outside the quarantine room wouldn't have gone unnoticed.

The commander sits down in the large chair by the main security control unit. "Your uncle has given his blessing?"

"Yes, sir."

Now it's his turn to laugh. "After fourteen years I finally get a *sir* out of you."

I try to hand him back the necklace, but he shakes his head. "Keep it. You may need it."

Finley opens his mouth as if to argue, but his dad shoots him a look and he closes it again.

"Thank you again, sir," I say. I honestly believe my voice

is sounding more respectful by the minute. "I know it might be a while, but will you let me know when the next ship heading to Earth arrives?"

The commander nods. "It may be more than a while, I'm sorry to say. Prince John has just put a halt on interstellar travel to or from Earth for any ship that didn't originate from there. That will lessen your chances by a considerable amount."

My stomach twists as he flicks on a digi-pen and a screen fills the space between us. "There are only two Earth-based airships off-planet currently. One is the *Royal Horizon*, which as you know is headed out of the solar system. The other is currently in the Gamma Quadrant and won't be back this way for six months."

"Six months!"

" 'Fraid so," he says. "I'll let you know if anything changes."

I mumble a thank-you, and as I pass by, I drop the necklace into the commander's coat pocket. Consider it my final magic trick.

I then walk slowly from the room. I'm not in any hurry to tell Marian about this giant setback. She may as well still go on her trip to Earth Beta. She'd make it back home quicker that way.

I haven't made it more than a few yards down the corridor before Finley comes rushing up behind me. He pulls me aside and whispers, "I have a way to get you to Earth. I said I owed you one, so this will make us even."

"That would make us more than even, Finley."

He leans closer. "Your only chance will be to leave while the *Royal Horizon* is still docked here. It will block the view in case anyone is looking, and their signal will block the radar, too."

I glance back at the command center to make sure the door is shut. "I appreciate the help, Finley, but you heard your dad. There aren't any Earth ships heading toward us, and the only other ship on Delta Z besides the *Royal Horizon* is Shane's shuttlecraft, and I already asked him."

Finley shakes his head. "That's not the only other ship on Delta Z."

CHAPTER TWELVE

Marian

The guest quarters here aren't as fancy as my bedroom at home, but they're comfortable enough, with soft blankets and a holo-picture over the dresser of an ocean lapping against a beach. I find myself entranced by it, admiring how the water leaves imprints in the sand as it roars in and retreats, over and over. At home all of the images of how the earth used to be have been destroyed, or at least hidden away. No one wants the constant reminder of what we've lost. Up here, though, they must not think of it that way.

Sarena knocks on my door and comes in without waiting for my reply. Lying to my classmates wasn't easy. I couldn't tell them the real reason, though, and risk them getting in trouble simply for their knowledge. Gareth and Asher tried to convince me that I'll get over the homesickness as soon as our journey continued and we got busier. Sarena was quiet, watching me steadily with her dark eyes.

"I know why you're really not coming with us," she says now, plopping down on the edge of the bed.

I keep unpacking my large suitcase, trying to keep my hands steady. "You do?"

She nods. "It's because of Robin."

I rest my pajamas on the pile and look up. "Robin?"

"I've seen how you two look at each other. Like love at first sight."

I laugh at that. "He tried to grab my suitcases at first sight. That's hardly love."

"Believe me," she says, "I remember. My arm still aches. And look!" She pushes up her sleeve to reveal a widening splotch of purple and blue on her skin.

I gasp. "What *is* that?"

She smiles. "It's a bruise! Without the medi-bots, this is what happens when we get hit — or, in my case, when someone backs into us!"

Fascinated, I reach to touch it with one finger. "Look at all those colors!"

Sarena pulls back. "It's pretty, but it does hurt a little."

"Sorry!" I say.

She twists her arm around to see it better. "Actually, I think it's kind of interesting." She rolls down her sleeve and looks up at me. "It's not so bad up here, you know, where our every move isn't monitored?"

I nod in agreement. "I'd miss the medi-bots, but I wouldn't miss the grid, that's for sure."

"Marian," she says, turning serious. "Whatever you're doing, be careful."

I don't answer. How can I? I can't promise anything.

"When are you leaving?" she asks.

I shake my head. "It could be a while before the right ship comes along."

"You sure you'll be okay up here alone after we leave? No offense, but before this trip I don't think I ever saw you outside the classroom without your maid or your mother accompanying you."

She's right, of course. I've never been on my own before, except for the night of the break-in, but I can't very well tell her about that.

She tilts her head at me with a sly smile. "Although you won't *be* alone, will you? You'll have Robin to look after you."

I throw the nearest item of clothing at her, which happens to be my nightgown. I have to admit, though, that doesn't sound like a bad way to pass the time. I could always beat him at a few more archery games!

"Wake up! We have to leave." Even though we only just met, I recognize Robin's voice shaking me out of a deep sleep. Turns out sleeping in an unfamiliar place isn't that hard after all.

I sit up in bed. "Lights!" I demand. But the lights don't turn on. I call out again, louder. "Lights!"

Robin laughs and switches on the light from the wall. "Even when you're shouting, it sounds like singing. Does yelling at the lights make them work on Earth?"

I cross my arms. "As a matter of fact, it does. And didn't anyone ever teach you it's not polite to barge into someone's room uninvited?"

"I'm pretty sure I knew that, but this couldn't wait until morning. We have to leave tonight. *Now*, actually. I found us another ship — and we can only take it while the *Royal Horizon* is still docked. Captain Pratchett is apparently ready to continue your journey, as is your ship. Figures this is the one time Shane actually worked quickly on a project. They must have been paying him well."

I hurry out of bed and begin grabbing clothes from the drawers and shoving them back into the suitcase. I needn't have bothered unpacking.

"There's more," he says. "The ship we'll be taking has no record anymore, although it once belonged to people from Earth. We won't be expected, and chances are, we won't be welcome. From what you've told me, you are well known. You should wear a disguise."

I stop tossing my clothes and turn around. "Did you say we? *We* won't be expected? You're coming with me?"

He nods. "I am. I mean, if you'll have me. Seems like I do unselfish things now. The last one paid off with a ship! Who knew?!"

I realize now that it was crazy to think I could do this alone. "Yes," I say. "I shall allow you to come with me."

He doesn't reply right away, and I worry I've misspoken. Then his eyes twinkle, and he laughs.

I laugh, too, relieved. "Now what did you say about a disguise?"

He surveys my clothes and shoes. "Looks like you have enough stuff here for six girls. Have you been seen in all these clothes?"

I nod. It would be too embarrassing to admit it's not unusual for me to wear three or four different outfits over the course of a day.

He glances over at the small suitcase on the floor by the closet. Ivy's suitcase. I haven't even opened it.

"Anything new in that one?"

"It belongs to my maid. She decided not to come at the last minute." Ivy wouldn't mind if I opened it, yet it still feels like an invasion of her privacy. Most people don't think of robots as needing or deserving privacy, but I've never thought of her as a robot. She's simply . . . Ivy. The girl who takes care of me.

I flip open the lid. One crisp top, one skirt, one pair of pants, one pair of thick-soled shoes. That's all she brought for three months away. I rub the collar of her uniform between my fingers. It makes me miss her. Even the mindless gossiping. She'd be asking me a hundred questions about Robin if she were here. I suddenly get an idea.

"I could dress as a maid," I tell him. "On Earth, all the maids are robots. It's a very respectable and important job, but an invisible one. I bet I could walk past my own parents in Ivy's uniform and they wouldn't notice me."

"Sounds perfect. I'll be outside. Fast would be good." He hurries out, leaving me to dress myself for the first time I can remember.

Donning the top of the maid uniform is easy, at least, with no complicated straps or hooks to fumble with. I've chosen to wear the pants and my own boots, leaving the skirt and shoes in the case. Braiding my own hair proves impossible, so I just twist it together and pin it back. Grandmother and Ivy would no doubt cringe if they saw the final, messy result.

I quickly determine that I'd like to travel lighter this time. I add a few pairs of underwear and socks to Ivy's suitcase, and as plain a top as I can find. I find my eyes keep darting to the center of the room, waiting for my daily schedule to appear. How strange it is not to know what the day will bring, and even stranger to think of the things you miss once they're gone, even if you thought you didn't like them.

"Before the sun goes supernova, please," Robin calls to me through the door.

"Almost ready." I fold a nightgown around Grandmother's headpiece, then add the bundle to the suitcase. I use my digi-pen to send Sarena an audio message that the rest of my belongings are now hers, grab my traveling cloak and the small suitcase, and hurry out to whatever's waiting on the other side of the door.

* * *

Turns out what's waiting is a two-person ship called the *Solar Hammer 2000*, which has apparently been hidden in the bowels of the spaceport for over a decade. "Amazing, isn't she?" Robin beams with pride at the ship, as though he built it with his own hands.

"It's . . . pretty small." And by *pretty small*, I mean it could fit into my bedroom at home. It's barely tall enough to stand up in. "Is it a short-range shuttlecraft?"

He shakes his head. "It's a state-of-the-art mini airship, complete with a homing device, whisper-quiet propulsion, light-speed technology, comet and asteroid warning system, and shields, of course. And it's all gassed up with high-octane Aloxxite, enough fuel to get us to Earth and back ten times. What it lacks in size, it makes up for in speed."

"And no one will miss it?"

"Only the commander and his son seem to know it's here. It was abandoned a long time ago. They've kept it in case of an emergency and never needed to use it. We'll just use the homing device to send it back up here when we arrive on Earth. The commander might not even notice it's missing."

He yanks open the door to the cockpit. "Ladies first."

I take a deep breath, tell myself it's only a few hours' journey, and climb in. This isn't one of those occasions where the space looks bigger on the inside than it does from the outside. If anything, it looks smaller. This isn't helped by the fact that all of Robin's boxes are piled in the back, filling most of the cargo space. "I couldn't leave them," he explains, sliding into the pilot's seat beside me. "Plus, you never know. We might need some of these things to barter with when we get there."

I nod. "Smart." I scan the dashboard in front of us. It's full of knobs and levers, one red button, and a lot of silver ones. At home, the elevators in each building only had one red button, too. "You sure you know how to fly this thing?"

"I totally don't," Robin admits. "But I have help coming right about now."

As he says it, three faces appear at his window. Finley, who led us to the arcade yesterday, Will, and a shorter, curly-haired boy I don't recognize. They're all wearing green pajamas and slippers.

Robin hops out and the curly-haired boy jumps in. "I'm Elan," he says. "I'm the smart one."

"Um, nice to meet you."

"You have the coordinates?" he asks, holding out his hand.

I dig out the folded paper from its usual spot in my boot and hand it to him. Like Robin and me before him, he rubs the paper between his fingers. Then he holds it up to his nose and sniffs it. "Interesting," he says. "I hadn't expected paper to smell so much like feet."

I redden. Perhaps I need to find a better place to keep it.

He rests the paper on his knee and then presses a button on the dashboard. A keypad slides out. It takes about five minutes for him to type in all the numbers, letters, and symbols. He double-checks it twice before sliding the keypad back in and handing me back the coordinates. "You're good to go."

"That's it?" I ask. "We just sit back and the ship sends us to King Ri — um, I mean, to our destination on Earth?"

"Yup. But whatever you do, don't press the big red button."

My eyes widen. "Why? What does that do?"

He shrugs. "No idea. I've just always wanted to say that."

He climbs out, leaving the door open behind him. I hear Finley tell Robin to return the ship without a scratch. Robin says he'll do his best and thanks the older boy. He shakes Elan's hand, and then only he and Will are left on the platform. Will hands Robin a cloak and says, "Dad wanted to make sure you had this cloak. Guess it was his from before he came here. It's for the cold. Or rain. Or for whenever it's not exactly seventy degrees all the time like up here." Robin thanks him and Will wipes away a tear even though he pretends he's scratching his cheek.

My stomach clenches as it hits me how big a deal this is for Robin. He's leaving a place he's lived his whole life to fly off into space with a girl he hardly knows, all to try to rescue a king who may or may not actually be in trouble. How will I ever repay such a gesture?

When Robin leans over to hug his cousin goodbye, I see his hand dart out and drop one of the gold chains into the pocket of Will's pajamas. I think Robin's a more thoughtful person than he would have others believe.

A few minutes later, we've managed to find the right buttons to open the exit hatch, start the nearly soundless engine, and float out into the dark of space. We both turn to look behind us as the hatch slides closed. "Well, that's that, then," Robin says, almost to himself. Then he adds, "Finley told me to stay in the shadow of the *Royal Horizon* as long as possible."

I try to focus on his words so I don't think about how tiny our ship is and how huge outer space is, and the fact that my hands are tingling. I slide down in my seat until my face lines up with a shiny panel on the dashboard. Seeing my reflection calms me, as usual, even though my brow is all pinched together. It grounds me.

"You okay?" Robin asks. "We've almost cleared the wake zone around the station. We'll be able to switch on the autopilot and accelerate soon."

His voice sounds calm, but his face is as pinched as mine.

I nod as we slip alongside, and then quickly past, the *Royal Horizon*. Our ship looks like something the *Horizon* sneezed out.

"Okay," he says. "Ready?"

I nod, or at least, I try to. I'm not sure my head actually moves. His finger presses the button beside the words *To Destination*. He then places his hand on top of my clenched ones and holds it there as the stars around us suddenly begin zooming past. It takes a few seconds for my brain to catch up and realize we're the ones moving faster, not the stars. Faster, even, than the trip here in the *Horizon*. At this rate, we'll get to Earth in no time.

After a few minutes where we haven't exploded or gotten an angry message from the commander demanding our return, we both visibly relax. We even joke about how it's a good thing we're going so fast because this thing has no bathroom.

Robin shows me how to trick someone into picking whatever card you want them to from his plastic card deck. I've never heard of a magic trick before, so it takes me a while to catch on to what he's doing. Then I laugh with delight as he makes one of the cards disappear and reappear in my messy half braid.

More time passes, and when I don't see the sun approaching, I start shifting in my seat. I notice Robin glancing back and forth between the coordinates and the view outside.

"Hmm," he finally says.

I don't like the sound of that *hmm*. "Everything okay?" I ask, trying to keep my voice light.

"I'm sure it is. I mean, I hope so. About how long did it take you to get to Delta Z in the *Royal Horizon*?"

I can only guess. "Maybe a few hours? I was kind of stuck to the window."

"Hmm," he says again. It sounds even worse the second time. "If this ship goes faster than the *Horizon*, we should have gotten to the inner solar system a while ago."

"Guess we didn't pass it by mistake?" I ask.

"Not a chance," he says. "Even though I've never seen it before, pretty sure we'd notice the giant yellow ball of gas in front of us."

"We must have gone off course, then," I suggest. "Maybe while a jack of clubs was being pulled out of my hair."

"Glad you still have your sense of humor." He checks and double-checks the coordinates in comparison with our current location. "Still heading to our destination."

We grow quiet.

After a few more minutes without the scenery changing, he asks, "When you overheard Prince John, did you definitely hear him say that King Richard was on Earth?"

"I certainly thought so," I reply.

Robin takes one more look out the front, sides, and behind us before saying, "I don't know where your coordinates are taking us, but it's *not* Earth."

CHAPTER THIRTEEN

⇜ Robin ⇝

The next hour feels like ten. I'm trying my best to comfort Marian, but I'm not sure it's working. She keeps clenching and unclenching her hands, and every few minutes she checks her face in the reflection of the dashboard when she thinks I'm not looking. She shouldn't worry; she's just as beautiful in the middle of outer space as she was on Delta Z.

Oh man, even Will would make fun of me for being so corny.

Everything has moved so quickly since her arrival that I haven't had a second to think about the hugeness of what I'm doing. Now we have plenty of seconds. Too many seconds. And all I'm doing is thinking. What if Prince John wrote down fake coordinates that don't actually lead anywhere? Or, worse yet, will lead us out of the galaxy, where even our full tank of Aloxxite won't be able to get us back? The other option — that they're real — isn't much better. Going to Earth — a planet I'd always been grateful not to live on — was crazy enough, but at least it was close by, and I'd be going with a native. None of the other known habitable planets have fared much better than Earth. Sure, some still have a few patches of land where things grow, and some managed to escape the devastation of wars, but most places these days don't take kindly to strangers.

I reach out and take Marian's hand in mine again. She squeezes back.

Finally, FINALLY, something changes outside the window. The darkness around us is lightening up ever so slightly. I check the dashboard screen. We're out of light speed! With no warning, a brightness the likes of which I've never seen surrounds our tiny ship, instantly blinding us.

We fling our hands in front of our eyes. I press my palms down hard, trying to quell the searing pain. "Wha — what was that?"

"It was a star," she replies. "We flew extremely close to it. Space lit up like that on the *Royal Horizon* when we passed the sun, but not nearly as bright. The ship must have had shields up to protect our eyes."

"Is it bright like this on Earth?" I ask, unable to move my hands away. If she says yes, it'll be a good reason to be glad we're not landing there.

"No," she says. "It lights everything up, but as long as you don't look right up at it, the sun is only a small yellow ball in the sky. I mean, that's what it's like on Earth, at least . . ." Her voice trails away at the end, and I'm guessing she has the same worries that I do about where we're heading.

"We're past it now," Marian tells me, resting her hand on my arm. "I think you can open your eyes."

Slowly, I lower my hands and blink away the black spots floating across my vision. My eyes still ache, but the brightness has dimmed enough that the pain is bearable. The light illuminates the scene around us, and I realize the view has changed again. Our ship whizzes by a large planet, and then a series of tiny ones. None of these constellations look like any I've learned about, and my teacher is very thorough. "I don't think this part of space has been explored yet," I tell her.

"I'm so sorry, Robin," she says miserably. "The coordinates were obviously wrong, or fake, or don't mean what we think they mean. Maybe Prince John just wanted to trick his staff into thinking he was holding King Richard somewhere. Maybe it's just a bluff to show how much control he has. Whoever had me steal the coordinates was fooled, too."

Her theory made sense. I wish I'd thought of it before suggesting this trip. I'll bet she did, too. "It's not your fault," I assure her.

We're slowing down further. We stare, transfixed, as a planet appears in the distance. Then the not-so-far distance, as we are suddenly nearly on top of it. The ship banks to the right and begins a trajectory to the dark side of the planet.

"We're going to land!" she exclaims. Then she gulps and adds, "On a planet that no one has heard of, hundreds of light-years away from our own solar system, where we may not be able to breathe the air."

We reach for each other's hands as the *Solar Hammer 2000* slows once again. The planet is still much too far away to reveal any surface details, but I don't see any control tower beacons, grids of city lights, or any satellites in orbit that we'd have to avoid smacking into. If there are people below us, I don't think they have technology yet.

"Don't worry," I tell her in as brave a voice as I can muster. "The autopilot will get us down to the surface safely. Then we'll simply activate the homing device to bring us right back to Delta Z. You'll be able to continue your journey with your classmates to Earth Beta, and I'll . . . well, I'll come visit you there." I grin. "I'm getting the hang of this space travel thing."

She smiles back, her face relaxing for the first time in hours. "Quite the adventure, at least, right?"

"Definitely," I reply, my mood also lifting considerably. "Everything is going to be fine."

"Yes," she agrees. "Better than fine."

Then the autopilot shuts off.

Turns out that a strange calm overtakes you when faced with your almost certain death as your tiny airship plummets toward the ground at two thousand miles per hour. Without the automatic guidance system, the ship is completely at the mercy of fate and gravity. And I don't think either of those are on our side right now.

"Um, any chance you know how to fly this thing?" The casual way Marian asks this tells me the same sense of calm has fallen upon her, as well. Either that or we've both descended into madness.

Dang my short attention span again! Why didn't I listen when the pilots talked to us? I'm pretty sure no sleight-of-hand magic trick or fancy unicycle maneuver is going to get us out of this one. Neither my charm, nor my skill with the hoverboard, or the sword, or the VR archery game is going to help, either.

But wait — maybe I do know something! BullsEye is right next to the VR Starfighter. I've played around with that one a few times while waiting my turn for the bow and arrow.

Marian is now gripping the sides of her seat, although she's trying to hide it. A sense of impending doom is chasing away my calm. My heart begins to pound as I desperately search the various screens on the dashboard in the hopes that something will look familiar. A lot of flashing lights and diagrams stare back at me. The speed indicator reads 420 knots. I have no idea if that's too fast or too slow. Plus, it doesn't really matter. The planet is so close now that I can see land and water formations. I'd calculate impact at thirty seconds or less. It's now or never.

First I stab at the autopilot button, trying to get it to turn back on. I'm not surprised when that fails. I know from the VR flying game that the circular object directly in front of me that looks like a miniature steering wheel is called a yoke. In the game I use that to move the ship up and down. I grit my teeth and grab onto it with both hands. Yanking it toward me has the immediate effect of causing the airship to jerk and buck while emitting an unpleasant hissing sound. Marian yelps, then clamps her mouth shut.

I let up on the yoke and grab the lever that sticks out halfway between us. The name for it comes to me as I pull down on it. *Throttle.* We finally slow down a small amount. But now we're zigzagging across the sky in a dizzying back-and-forth pattern.

"I'll take the stick thingy," Marian says, reaching for the throttle. "You do the wheel thingy."

I nod. Our hands collide briefly as I release the throttle and she grabs it. For a few seconds, neither of us moves our hands. Then I reluctantly move my hands back up to the yoke.

Between Marian controlling our speed, and me doing my best to keep us steady, we manage to cross into the planet's atmosphere without spinning out of control. From here, the light reflecting off the planet's three moons is more than enough to reveal the features on the surface. And what it reveals — in between large bodies of water and smaller ones — is a dense dead zone, just like on Earth and the other known habitable planets where the people have killed off their forests. Good thing we plan to leave here as soon as we can. All I can do is try to steer us toward a safe landing in a clearing.

If I can find one.

I glance at Marian. She's checking out the landscape, too, and her brows are furrowed. Then she turns and says hurriedly, "You know, we don't actually have to land now. The autopilot isn't in control anymore, so we can just turn around right now! Right?"

"Yes! Let's do that." Hope flairs up in both of us as we get to work pulling and yanking and twisting.

It takes us only a few seconds to realize it's too late. The gravitational pull of the planet has our ship firmly in its grasp. We're not going fast enough to break away, and there's no way to get up enough speed to turn before striking the planet. Anything we do barely nudges us off our course. In an unspoken agreement, we stop fighting it. I point toward what looks to be a small patch of dark ground without any of the tall spiky things in the way. I barely have time to register that I'm about to see trees for the first time — even dead ones — before our ship is skimming the tops of them.

Marian pulls on the throttle with all her might, and I use all my flying skills to keep us from hitting the trees. But really, VR Starfighter isn't my game. I manage to hit every third tree or so, but we barely feel it. The clearing is coming up fast, and the ship's headlights reveal it's more water than land. Still, it's better than crashing into a tree and breaking into a million tiny shards. But at this speed, the ground is going to be just as hard and will do just as much damage if we can't slow down enough.

"How do we engage the shields?" Marian shouts.

Shields! Yes! We need those! For once the solution comes easily. To the left of the yoke is a picture of the ship in a bubble. I take my hand off the yolk for a split second to press the button. Nothing happens. Then Marian points out her window, where we're still skimming trees. "Look at the branches!"

It takes a second to realize that the branches are now breaking off three feet or so away from the ship instead of directly hitting the ship. The shields are working!

I barely have time to rejoice at that small victory because five seconds later we hit the ground with a sickening thud, the rear of the ship hitting first, then the nose. We sink down in our seats, bracing ourselves as we bounce along the ground, skid on a shallow body of water, slide on a sludgy mixture of earth and water, and finally screech to a stop. Our view out the front window is totally obscured by dirt and debris, which makes me think the front end of the ship is buried in the ground. We'll have to dig ourselves out before we activate the homing device and head back to Delta Z.

"Are you okay?" I quickly ask as I fling off my seat strap. I hadn't realized how much it had been digging into my chest and stomach.

Marian hesitates a second, then nods. "I mean, we did just crash-land on a strange planet — but yeah, I think I'm okay. You?"

I make a show of feeling my arms, legs, and torso, then quickly pat my face. "Phew, my best feature survived unharmed."

She looks at me and bursts out laughing. "How do you know your face is your best feature? What if your best feature is your left elbow? Or your belly button?"

I shake my head. "My belly button's pretty ugly." Soon we're laughing so hard we're gasping for breath. It's obvious we're laughing because we've just survived the scariest experiences of our lives, but man, it feels good.

We eventually stop and gather our wits about us, wiping our cheeks and surveying the damage. The ship has gone totally dark, no headlights anymore, no flashing lights, just a faint clicking sound. I poke and prod, but only one gauge flickers — the one that says *Low Fuel*, with a series of numbers running below it. We must have damaged the fuel tank as we landed and fuel leaked out. I lean forward to scrutinize the readout to see if I can make anything out of the numbers.

"Um, Robin?" Marian says, tugging at my sleeve. Her voice is higher pitched than usual, which only makes it sound more musical.

"Hmm?" I reply, my attention focused on the screen.

"You need to see this." The tugging continues until I finally look up. She's turned around in her seat, facing the cargo area. I swivel around, wincing as the yoke jams into my side. Not sure what could be so interesting back there. The only things behind us are the boxes.

Or, more accurately, the only things behind us WERE the boxes. Now there is only a huge, gaping hole and half a billion stars.

CHAPTER FOURTEEN

Marian

Everything we brought with us is gone. Robin's treasures from his parents. My jeweled headpiece from Grandmother. The laughter and relief I felt only moments ago after the relatively safe landing has vanished. Fear, dread, and regret are now competing to take their place. Even before Robin confirms it, I know this airship will never leave the ground. Even if we could somehow get the homing device to set a course for Delta Z, even if we could miraculously find more fuel, the ship is way too badly damaged to fly. We are stuck on this planet.

On the positive side, we can breathe the air here. The brisk night breeze rushing into the ship proves that. Beside me, Robin shivers and pulls his cloak closed. His teeth begin to chatter. This pulls me out of my dark thoughts a bit. "It's not *that* cold, Robin."

He flips up his hood and wraps his arms tighter around himself in response. Even in the moonlight, I can see his lips have gone blue. Guess life in a temperature-regulated space-port thins the blood.

"We're going to have to huddle together for warmth," I say. He doesn't complain as I move closer to him until we're leaning against the backs of the chairs, our legs curled under us.

"Any chance there's a tracking device on the ship?" I ask

hopefully. We may not be able to get ourselves off the planet, but maybe someone else will come rescue us.

He shakes his head.

I try again. "Maybe you gave a copy of the coordinates to someone before we left? Your uncle, or Will, or Elan? Even Finley?"

He shakes his head. "That would have been too smart. But even so, we went off course as soon as the autopilot shut off. We could be hundreds or even thousands of miles away from where those coordinates would have taken us."

Hope flickers away. He's right. And the people who sent me to get the coordinates likely realized right away that they were fake, so it's not like anyone from Earth will be showing up. If King Richard really *is* in danger, hopefully they will not give up on him. I'll never find out now who *they* are, or if they chose me because of who my father is, or because they saw something in me that I don't see.

One thing I *do* know is that Grandmother will never braid my hair again. A knot forms in my throat that makes it hard to swallow. I must have let a tear escape, because Robin's finger brushing my cheek startles me.

"Don't worry," he says. "We'll figure this out in the morning. Everything looks bleaker in the middle of the night." He pauses, then adds, "Except for the sky. The sky here is awesome."

I nod, not trying to speak yet. If I could make myself ignore all the unfamiliar sounds around us, I'd be better able to appreciate the show the sky is putting on for us. The *Royal Horizon* had been moving so fast that the stars were a blur of light. Even on Delta Z, they seemed to be in motion, since the spaceport was in orbit. But from the planet's surface, the stars are frozen in place, glittering like diamonds. Every few seconds one streaks by.

But as it is, I'm finding it hard to ignore the thumping of branches and the rushing of the wind through the husks of the trees, interrupted by the occasional distant screech or howl. There's also a rhythmic, high-pitched hum that I'd assumed was coming from the ship, but now I'm no longer sure. "I never thought the Dead Zone would be so noisy," I say to Robin. "From The City it sounds completely, well, *dead*."

"I don't think we're in a dead zone after all," he says. "Did you see any signs of civilization when we flew overhead?"

I think about this for a minute, then shake my head. "I wasn't really looking, though."

"How about when you left Earth, could you see your city from high above it?"

I nod. "When we first entered outer space I could still see the lights."

"That's what I figured." He inches closer to the opening, where a gust of wind has sent some broken twigs scuttling across the floor. He picks one up and brings it over. "I think we're actually in the woods, like the *living* woods. With green trees and fresh soil that plants and vegetables can grow in. Maybe even animals live here." I can hear the excitement in his voice.

He places the twig in my hand. Soft triangular-shaped objects protrude from the sides in an uneven pattern. My eyes open wide as I realize what I'm feeling. *Leaves!* Living leaves, flexible and healthy, not stiff and charred like the ones that occasionally float into The City and crumble to bits under your fingers. Without thinking, I scramble to my feet and race toward the gap in the ship. Robin yanks me back before I get to the edge.

"Not so fast," he says, holding on to my sleeve. "You heard the part about the animals, right?"

"I did — and Robin, if there's vegetation, there could be bunnies! Bunnies!"

He raises one eyebrow and tilts his head at me. "Bunnies?"

I cup my hands like I'm holding and petting a small creature. "So soft and cute with those twitchy little noses."

"How do you know what their noses look like?" he asks, tilting his head at me.

I give a small smile as the memory floats back to me. "Actually, it was King Richard. When I was little, he used to tell us stories about a family of bunny rabbits who lived in a hollow tree. Now I'll get to see a real bunny AND a real tree!" I take another step toward the exit, but he holds firm. I sigh. "Yes?"

"Do you know stories about any *other* animals?" he asks.

I consider the question and shake my head. "Not really. The teachers aren't supposed to tell us about nature. Prince John doesn't want anyone to think life was any different than it is. But now . . ." I gesture to the opening in the ship. "Now we can find out for ourselves!" I start to pull away again, eager to explore.

"Marian," Robin says calmly, still holding me firmly. It's starting to get a little annoying. "It's the middle of the night. Not all animals are fluffy little bunnies. There are others who could outrun you, outclimb you, then tear you limb from limb and pick at your bones and you wouldn't even see them coming."

My eyes widen. "Oh. Right." I sit back down. "Perhaps we'll stay here, then."

We take our mind off the situation by pointing out patterns of stars. My favorite is a constellation with especially bright stars in the shape of an arrow that Robin names Mister Pointy. Eventually our throats grow hoarse and our eyes droop. We slip off our shoes and wrap our cloaks around us like blankets.

I awaken to the sunlight pressing against my eyes. I rub my eyelids, then open them. The gap in the ship reveals a mossy forest full of green leaves and brown tree trunks so spectacularly beautiful that I gasp. Out of the corner of my eye, I can see that Robin is still asleep beside me, his cloak rising and falling with each shallow breath. He needs to see this. I reach over and shake him, but he just mutters, "Not time for school yet, Will. I'm having a really good dream."

I force myself to look away from the splendor outside to fully turn in his direction. I yank back my hand, jump up, and smack my head right on the ceiling.

We've got company.

My head contacting the ceiling is enough to finally wake Robin. He groans and throws his hands over his eyes. "So bright. Turn it off."

Like I can turn off the sun. "You have a bigger problem," I reply in a whisper.

"Why are you whispering?" he asks as he pulls his hood farther down over his eyes. "And why is my left foot wet?"

"Um, I think you need to see for yourself," I reply, not moving anything other than my lips.

He groans again, but peels his hands from his eyes and leans up on his elbows. His whole body goes rigid with fear.

I don't blame him. If a wild beast was licking *my* foot I'm sure I'd have the same stunned look on my face.

Although really, the beast *is* kind of cute. Long gangly limbs, big furry ears, and the deepest brown eyes I've ever seen. A random pattern of white dots run down its brown back and onto its swishing tail. No doubt sensing Robin's fear, the animal looks up, right into his eyes. The two of them stare at each other for what feels like a really long time. Then the creature takes a step closer to Robin, bends his head down, and nuzzles Robin's hand. I can't take it anymore — I melt. "He likes you! You've made a friend!"

Robin slowly moves his hand away from the animal's nose. I guess he might not *want* an animal friend. But instead of pulling his hand back under his cloak, he reaches above the animal's head and pets it! This goes on for so long that my stomach begins to grumble. It's been a very long time since my last full meal.

"Um, sorry to break up the start of a lovely friendship between you and the beast of the jungle, but we should find something to eat. And I need to, um, you know." My face reddens.

"It's a deer," he says, his voice full of awe. "Pretty sure it's a girl deer, and those dots means she's still a baby." He clears his throat. "And yeah, I need to 'you know,' too."

We slip on our boots while the animal called a deer watches calmly, nudging Robin's legs. Robin stretches out his other hand toward me. "Ready?"

I sprint past him and jump through the hole out into the tall, glorious grass. "Ready!"

He laughs and jumps out after me. The deer hops down after him, then curls up at the base of our ship. We run around in the grass like fools. It's scratchy on my legs, but I don't mind. We toss soft leaves into the air and at each other, and bend down to smell flowers growing wild on the bushes. Real bushes, not ones made of foam. Robin's teeth are still chattering in the early morning chill, and his eyes are still watering from the sun, but he doesn't seem to mind. "Look!" he shouts, pointing up in the air. "Birds!"

My head flies back so fast I've likely done serious damage to my neck. I wait a few seconds for the medi-bots to go to work, but when the discomfort doesn't subside, I decide that Robin is correct about there being no technology on this planet, or at least no medi-bots, which means if I get hurt, I have to heal the old-fashioned way. And no electricity also means no tracking grid! I'll gladly put up with a sore neck for the freedom now afforded me!

I turn in circles, staring up at the sky until I spot them myself. *Birds!* Three flying creatures swoop over our heads, wings flapping as they dart from branch to branch. Robin and I meet each other's eyes and whoop as we run underneath them, flapping our arms. I don't think I've ever had so much fun. Our deer looks up at us lazily, then seems to shrug as she rests her head again. Guess birds are nothing new to her.

I finally tear my eyes away from their flight in time to see Robin yank a tiny blue ball from a bush. Before I can stop him, he pops it in his mouth. I hold my breath, afraid he's going to keel over dead from eating something poisonous. But his face splits into one of his big, lopsided grins. He pulls more off the bush and runs over, holding his cupped hands up to my face. "You have to try this!"

Between his excitement and my grumbling stomach, I can't refuse. I take one in my hand, and immediately liquid squishes out all over my fingers as the tiny ball flattens. Robin laughs and hands me another one. "Gentle."

I try again, this time getting the ball all the way onto my tongue before breaking it open. Now it's my turn to grin with delight. No doubt little pieces of blue skin are caught in my teeth. Mother would definitely scold me for doing something so unladylike. Never did I guess that food could taste like this. Food that grows from a PLANT. In the DIRT. I swallow and hold out my hand. "More, please."

We run from bush to bush, pulling them off and tossing them into our mouths. Robin feeds some to our new friend, too. I can't help noticing how gentle he is with the deer. It makes me like him even more. Unable to wait any longer, we head in opposite directions and duck behind the biggest trees we can find.

I now have a new appreciation for my bathroom at home.

I'm heading back toward the yummy bushes when my foot lands on something hard and flat. I push aside some fallen leaves and dig my fingers into the dirt (SUCH a nice feeling!) until I've revealed something I never thought I'd see again. "Hooray!" I shout, holding up my (Ivy's) suitcase! It's dented and banged up, but the lock still holds. A quick shake lets me know my headpiece and clothes are still in there. I sit back on my heels, grateful and relieved.

We spend the next hour or so covering the area in a circle around the ship, never letting it — or each other — out of our sights. Just because our baby deer is friendly, we're not taking any chances on the others. Not too far from the ship, we find a small stream and greedily cup our hands and drink. It's crisp and refreshing and tastes a little sharp, not anything like the bland, overprocessed "water" we get at home. There must be metal still in this planet's soil!

Our widening search reveals a few more of our lost items: one silver dagger, the small golden statue I'd seen on the holo-screen, another even smaller marble statue of what I now know is a bird, and a thin gold chain with a single white ball dangling from it. Robin says the ball is a pearl and that it grew under the sea. He knows a lot more words for things in nature than I do for someone who grew up in a completely artificial environment. Much to our delight, Robin pulls his funny hat with the feather out of the mud (that's what he calls the mixture of water and earth). It's all squished and dirty, but a few dips in the stream and it's as good as new. Except wet. He lays it out in the sun to dry, right next to the deer.

"I think we should give her a name," he says, patting the deer on the top of her head. "Like Nosey. Or Spots."

I laugh. "Those are names?"

He crosses his arms dramatically. "You've got better ones?"

I think for a minute. I've never named anything in my life, but I want to try. "How about naming her after your home?" I suggest. "We could call her Delta Deer, or Deedee for short."

He relaxes his stance. "Yeah, that's pretty good." Turning to the animal, he says, "So, Deedee, are you the only ground-dwelling creature on this planet of yours, or are there others?"

"Like bunnies," I add.

As though in response to Robin's question, Deedee's ears shoot up. She bolts off down the length of the stream, faster than I'd have guessed those skinny legs could go. Robin and I look at each other. "Was it something I said?" Robin asks.

I giggle (apparently I've become the kind of girl who giggles) and joke, "Maybe she doesn't like her name. Maybe yours are better." As we run after her, I call out, "How about Miss Nosey Spots? Or, wait — *Princess* Nosey Spots?" Now we're both giggling as we run. I think all this actual fresh air filled with real plant-generated oxygen is making both of us a little loopy, but in a good way.

Deedee doubles back, and when she finally stops, her ears stand straight up, and she paws at the ground nervously. She's standing only a few feet away from the base of the tree where we'd left the few possessions that had survived the crash.

And she's not alone.

CHAPTER FIFTEEN

⤙ Robin ⤚

"I don't think they've spotted us," I whisper. I flip up the hood of my cloak and gesture for Marian to do the same. She's frozen in place, her left foot hovering in the air. I quickly count five men of varying ages on the other side of the stream. Two have long brown hair, one is yellow-haired like Marian, and two are quite short and totally bald. I peg those two as brothers.

Marian silently lowers her foot onto the grass and whispers, "Maybe we should just ask them for help. *People* mean *towns*, and *towns* mean *places to eat*, and maybe even someone to fix our ship."

"Yes," I whisper back without taking my eyes from them, "but they might not be the friendly type. They look a little rough-and-tumble, if you know what I mean."

The group is close enough now for their words to float over to us. "The sheriff's prize is mine this year," one of the bald men brags. "No one else can come close to me with a bow and arrow."

"Is that so?" another man growls. "I'll beat ya with my eyes closed."

A bow and arrow?

I risk a peek under the hood of my cloak to see who's speaking.

The first man jabs his finger into the other's chest. "That purse of silver coins is *mine*."

Deedee chooses this moment to try to cross the stream. Her hoof slips on a rock, and Marian and I cringe as a few of the men turn at the resulting splash.

"Look," the yellow-haired man shouts. He looks younger than the others by ten years or so. "It's one of the sheriff's deer! How'd it get all the way out here?"

The older man slaps him on the arm. "Why are you always asking dumb questions? It walked, that's how." The first pair is now rolling around on the ground, still arguing over who is better at archery. Watching them is making me miss Will and our wrestling matches.

"Let's go," Marian whispers. "We can't let them find the ship. They'll just fight over it."

We're only a few feet away from our belongings. In unspoken agreement, we slowly inch toward them, careful to avoid any twigs or crunchy leaves. I stuff my still-damp hat and the small statues in my cloak pocket and slip the dagger in my belt. I hand Marian the new gold chain. She tries to push it back in my hand, but I shake my head at her. It's best if we divide up the valuables. She opens her suitcase a crack and drops it in.

I glance behind us to see if the coast is clear. That's a mistake. Deedee catches my eye and makes a bleating sound. This time she bounds across the stream without slipping and heads right toward us! She must have liked the berries I gave her. *Berries!* That's what those blue balls are called.

"Shoo," I whisper, waving my hand for her to go back in the opposite direction. But Deedee only looks at me, sniffing the air. "Please, go away." Deedee actually takes a step backward, but it's too late. The men have stopped tumbling and shouting and have all turned to look in our direction. Two of the men reach for the swords at their sides.

"Hark!" one of them barks, drawing his sword in one swift movement.

"Who goes there?" the other adds, holding his hand above his brow to block the sun. "Who is hiding yonder beneath that hood?" I instinctively step in front of Marian. She immediately steps back beside me. *Stubborn.* At least she's doing a good job of hiding her suitcase behind her.

The man steps forward menacingly. "I ask one last time. Loosen your tongues or I will loosen them for you."

Now that doesn't sound like fun.

"We mean you no harm," Marian calls out.

The men stop and stare, no doubt as entranced as I was when I first heard her speak. Then all of them except the yellow-haired man begin to laugh. "You? Mean *us* harm? Haha haha."

Marian frowns.

The man wielding the sword takes another step closer, looking only at me this time. "What is your name? Who do you work for?"

I clear my throat and announce loudly, "I am Robin." Then, when that doesn't sound impressive enough, I lift my chin and add, "Robin of Locksley."

The men exchange looks and shake their heads. "That's not a name!" one of them shouts.

"His name certainly *is* Robin," Marian insists. "It's Robin . . ." Her eyes dart all around us until her gaze lands on my face, then my cloak. "*Hood.* His name is Robin Hood."

I groan and whisper out of the corner of my mouth, "Really? Robin Hood? What kind of name is *that*?"

She whispers back, "Be grateful you're not Princess Nosey Spots."

Can't argue with logic like that.

The man with the sword appraises me. "I do not believe I've heard of you, Robin Hood of Locksley. Why are you trespassing in the sheriff's woods? He doesn't take kindly to strangers. And you're mighty strange, with your green clothes and your skin pale like a ghost. Are you a ghost, kid?"

I shake my head. "We're only passing through," I assure him. "We'll be on our way now." I take Marian's arm and we begin walking as quickly as we can in the opposite direction of our ship. Deedee steps out of the shadow of the trees and trots along beside us.

From out of nowhere, an arrow whizzes past my head and impales a tree trunk three feet ahead of me. Then another one, and another. Marian yelps. I whirl around to see if she's hurt, heart pounding. She holds up her hands. "I'm fine," she says in a high voice. "Just a close one." Relieved, and then furious, I stomp toward the men, my dagger in my hand before I even realize I've pulled it out.

"Robin!" Marian hisses. "Don't!"

But I can't let it pass. I hadn't noticed anyone had a quiver of arrows, but now that I'm closer I see the two men who were bragging earlier about winning the sheriff's prize have them slung over their shoulders. If I weren't so furious, I'd be eager to examine their equipment to see how similar it is to its virtual counterpart.

"Why are you shooting at us?" I demand.

The men form a circle around me. Most of them are

taller by a foot. Perhaps I haven't thought this out too well. Still, I hold my ground. "You can't just go around shooting arrows at people for no reason," I argue. "You could have really hurt us."

The men growl. One replies, "If we wanted to hurt you, you'd already be bleeding."

"Yeah," another agrees. "The sheriff will want to do that himself."

This sheriff guy is sounding less and less like someone I want to hang around with. "He'd hurt me for walking through his woods?"

"Nah," the yellow-haired man says, speaking for the first time. "For that he'd just take all your money, your land, and your family. But for stealing one of his deer, that's a different story."

"Deer? I didn't steal any deer."

Marian clears her throat and points to my feet. I glance down, not wanting to take my eyes from the men for too long. Deedee is curled up by my left foot. She really likes that foot.

I give the men a weak smile. "Ah, *that* deer. We didn't know she belonged to anyone. And anyway, she found *us*, not the other way around."

The men just stare at Deedee, who has now begun to nuzzle my leg. I try to nudge her away, but she doesn't seem to get the message.

"There you are!" a deep voice calls out from the woods. My heart quickens at the thought that perhaps this is the sheriff himself, come to exact his revenge on the deer thieves. But when the man behind the voice appears, he's short and round, in long brown robes tied with a sash of yellow rope. He reminds me of the large-bellied statue from my parents. His haircut looks like someone put a bowl on his head and cut around it, then shaved off everything except the outside circle of the bowl. A strange look, but somehow on him it seems to work.

The men lower their weapons. "Friar Tuck," the tallest of the men says. "We thought you'd wandered off to town."

"Did you, now?" the friar replies, mopping his brow with a rag. "It felt more like you left me behind on purpose."

I take the distraction of the friar's arrival as our chance to leave. I signal to Marian with my eyes and then inch away from Deedee. I'm nearly out of the circle before one of the sword-bearers lowers his sword right in front of me.

"Not so fast. Is this your wife?" He tilts his head at Marian.

"My wife?" I repeat, stunned by the question. On Delta Z only the old people are married. "Of course not."

Marian makes a sound between a grunt and a laugh.

The man steps closer. "Your sister, then?"

My lips suddenly feel very dry. I'm not sure of the right answer.

Marian steps forward. "I'm Marian. His . . . his maid," she says, solving the problem for me. "See my outfit?" She slips off her cloak to reveal the maid uniform she's been wearing since we left Delta Z.

"You don't look like any maid *I've* ever seen," the man says with a snort.

"Well, that is what I am," she replies.

The friar stops cleaning his glasses with the sleeve of his robe, finally recognizing that there are strangers in his midst. He looks from Marian to me and then to the men surrounding us. To my surprise — and no doubt Marian's — he hurries over and takes her arm. "Ah, 'tis the lovely Maid

Marian, come to start her scholarly life at the monastery. We've been wondering when you'd arrive."

Marian stares at him, then gives a little curtsy kind of move that I've never seen her make before. "My name's not Maid Marian," she tells him gently. "I'm a maid named Marian. I, um, clean things?"

But the friar only pats her on the arm. "Nonsense, my dear. You have come to study the ancient ways, to transcribe the books, to paint and contemplate our beautiful world."

"Did you . . . did you say books?" Marian asks, eyes wide. "And *paint*?"

"Of course," the friar says. "You shall study all the arts." He turns to me. "Thank you, young man, for escorting our newest student through these woods. They can be quite dangerous for a young lady on her own." He looks pointedly at the group of men, half of whom have started fighting with one another again. "We'll be going now."

"Not so fast," the tallest guy says. He must be the leader. "These two stole one of the sheriff's deer. They must pay the consequences."

This is getting old. "I told you, we didn't steal her. You can take her right now."

One of the guys with the arrows nudges the other. "Could be good target practice for the contest."

The other considers this and grins. "Yeah, doesn't seem like it moves too quick."

It takes a few seconds for what he said to sink in. When it does, I immediately step in front of Deedee. "You can't use her for target practice! You said no one can harm the sheriff's deer!"

They laugh. The leader says, "We said *you* can't harm the sheriff's deer. *We* can do anything we want."

Now Marian is the one to step forward. "You are NOT going to hurt this deer."

"And who's going to stop me?" the leader asks, jeering. I hate that he's looking at her like that.

"How about we make a little bet?" I ask. I point to a narrow willow tree about two hundred feet away. "We draw a bull's-eye on that tree. If your two best shooters' arrows land closer to the center than mine, then you can have this deer and you'll get no trouble from us. If my arrow bests yours, then you will let us and the deer leave in peace. There are two of you, so I will get two tries."

The leader doesn't reply at first. We both know he has the upper hand here, whether he accepts the bet or not. My hope is that he'll be unable to pass up the challenge.

"You don't even have a bow," he finally points out.

"I'm certain you can let me borrow one, and two arrows to fit in it," I reply. "Your worst two arrows, no doubt."

"We want more when we win," the leader says. He gestures with one dirty thumb toward Marian. "My cousin here's in need of a wife."

The yellow-haired man — no doubt the cousin in question — blushes and kicks at the dirt. "C'mon, let's just leave 'em alone," he mutters. But no one pays attention.

"They'd make a lovely couple!" one of the men roars. They all laugh. This makes the cousin blush even deeper. "I'm sure the good friar could survive with one less student."

Friar Tuck opens his mouth to argue, but seems to sense he's pushed his luck far enough with this group.

I look at Marian. She narrows her eyes and gives me one curt nod. "Show 'em what you've got, Robin."

The archers' skills are stronger than I'd hoped. Both hit the tree, one coming only two inches from the center of the target that Friar Tuck — as the only neutral party — has hastily drawn on with chalk.

"Ha! Beat that!" they shout. One of the men hands me his bow and quiver. As suspected, the only arrows left are bent, with torn feathers and splintered tips. This doesn't worry me as much as they probably figured it would. In the VR archery game, after you level up a few times, your arrows begin to look like these. I've learned to adjust my aim.

I choose the one in the best condition and load it in the bow. It feels almost exactly the same as the virtual bow and arrow, except it doesn't click into place on its own. And the string is thinner and lighter. On second thought, it doesn't feel much the same at all. I pull back, close one eye, and aim. If I were to spare even a second to think about the consequences of losing, I'd never let the arrow fly. So I don't think about it.

Thwak!

The arrow swerves just as it approaches the target, knocking the first man's arrow to the ground. He stomps his foot. While everyone is oohing and aahing over that one, I shoot off the last arrow, which finds its mark directly in the center of the bull's-eye. I hand the bow back to the stunned archer. "We will be taking our leave of you now."

Before anyone can protest, I grab Marian's hand and we edge away from the group. I purposely head in the opposite direction from where we came. I don't want to risk leading them to the airship in case they follow us. Friar Tuck trails along, his expression a cross between relieved, surprised, and exhausted. I can't tell if he really believes Marian is his lost student, or if he's just trying to keep her safe. Either way, we're going to have to ditch him eventually. It's impossible to know who to trust here.

The men shout after us, but they don't appear to be pursuing. No one looks back, not even Deedee, who has, of course, tagged along. My plan is to wait for the men to move on, then double back and return to the relative safety of our ship. We can figure out the next step from there.

We don't get far along the path before we reach a fork. A wooden sign (real wood!) sticks out of the ground, announcing what lies in each direction. Both Marian and I reach our hands out to touch the wood. It's both rougher and smoother than I'd have thought.

Sherwood Village to the left, Sherwood Forest to the right.

"We go this way," Friar Tuck says, pointing left. "The school is in the hills above the village."

I glance at Marian, then tell the friar, "Thank you for helping us, but we can take it from here."

He shrugs. "Every man's path is his own. I wish you safe passage on yours."

"Thank you, sir," I reply.

The friar nods at Marian and turns toward the village.

"Please wait one more moment," Marian tells him, then pulls me aside. "What if we go with him to the school?" she whispers in an excited tone. "If we're going to be stuck here, we should learn all we can, right? They have books there — real books! And art, and paint, and —"

"But what about trying to get the ship repaired?" What I really want to ask is, *School? You want me to go to school when no one's forcing me to?*

"Robin, think about it. Half the ship's hull is torn off, and from what we can tell, this planet is still in its medieval period. They have steel and iron and silver, but nothing that could withstand the pressures of space travel. And they certainly don't have the capability to make Aloxxite. That airship's never leaving the ground."

I try to accept her words, but my brain won't seem to let me. Never in my wildest dreams did I imagine I'd ever get to see nature in all its glory, and I'm beyond grateful for the chance. But how can I just settle into life here without doing all I can to get us home? I'd never see Will and Uncle Kent again, or Shane. I might even miss Vinnie. Well, probably not Vinnie. But I'd never find out what happened to my parents, that's for sure. And I promised to return the *Solar Hammer*. That promise might not have meant much to me even a week ago, but it does now.

"I'm sorry, Marian," I tell her honestly. "I don't think we can give up without at least trying."

She searches my face, then says, "I understand." We hold each other's gaze here in the dense woods, where the birds cry out as they pass overhead.

Finally, Friar Tuck clears his throat and says, "I must be on my way. Meditation hour begins when the sun is directly overhead. I try never to miss it. The ability to look inside oneself for inner guidance and wisdom is vital to our growth as spiritual beings."

"Um, definitely," I reply, even though I have no idea what he's talking about. "Ready, Marian?" I step toward the opposite path. Deedee trots up to my side and waits.

But Marian doesn't join us. "Every man must choose his own path," she says softly but firmly. "So must every woman."

I don't think I like where this is headed. "What are you saying?"

She steps close and reaches out her hand toward me. She hesitates for a second, then rests it on my arm. "Robin, these few days since I left home have given me a freedom I never dreamed could exist. No mandatory shopping trips, no full schedule, no grid tracking my every move. I want to do what he said." She gestures to the friar, who is pretending to pull a splinter out of his finger. Or maybe he really is pulling a splinter out of his finger.

"I want to look inside myself," she continues. "I want to think, I want to learn and paint and read. I want to feed my brain. And if you *do* figure out a way to get the ship running, this could be my only chance to do any of those things."

I don't want her to go. But she seems so excited. We both know there's a better chance of us sprouting wings than getting that ship off the ground, but still, she's willing to let me try. Which means that I should be willing to let her go. I turn to the friar. "Can you guarantee her safety?"

"Can you?" he asks, not unkindly.

I want to say of course I can, but I'm pretty sure now that isn't true.

"I do not claim to guess where you two hail from," he says, "but here in Sherwood our school is the safest place, unless you have a home to return to?"

Neither of us responds. We both do — and don't — have homes.

"You'll come visit me," Marian says, not making it a question.

I push past the lump in my throat to reply, "Yes, of course."

She pulls me a little farther away from the friar. "Promise you'll be careful. No more rushing up to groups of strange men with daggers in your hand."

"Well, I can't promise that," I reply. "But now that I know we're not alone here, I won't let people sneak up on me. I'll walk with you as far as the village and look around for supplies there."

"Good. And also, you should put your hood down. You look like you're hiding something."

"But what's Robin Hood without his hood?" I joke, pushing it off my head. I've never felt wind in my hair before. Or any wind anywhere. It feels great.

A minute later I hear a slicing sound as an object whizzes through the trees a short distance behind us. I've heard that sound a million times in the archery game. Deedee and I stop short. I scan the woods but don't spot the man or the arrow he shot. Another *whoosh*, but still I spot no arrow. The men must be uncertain which way we went and are trying to draw us out. Marian and the friar have launched into a conversation about books and are strolling a few yards ahead.

I hurry to catch up. Marian has an excited smile on her face as the friar describes the kind of ink the scribes use on the parchment paper. She sure does love books. I wish I could be there when she sees her first one.

"Why don't you guys go on to the village?" I suggest, trying to sound casual so she doesn't worry that anything's wrong. I'm pretty certain once they make it out of the woods they'll be safe.

"I think I should" — I pause, then lower my voice so only she can hear —"check on the ship."

Her smile fades. "Are you certain?"

"Yes, you guys better hurry along so you're not late for . . . what was it? Feeding your brain?"

"Robin, I —"

There's no time. I hand her the small suitcase and squeeze her shoulder. I thank the friar and take off at a run back toward the fork in the road. I wish I had my hoverboard. No one could catch me then.

When I reach the signpost, I run as fast as I can down the opposite path, the one marked *SHERWOOD FOREST.* Then I pull my hat out of my pocket, straighten out the feather, place it on my head, and set about making enough noise for three people.

CHAPTER SIXTEEN

Marian

As soon as we enter Sherwood Village, the urge to run after Robin and give up this crazy idea loosens its grip on me. It's impossible not to get swept up by all the activity around us. Kids squeal as they run by, pushing barrels with a stick in some kind of race. Stalls and carts line the streets, filled with items I mostly don't recognize. I try to absorb all of it — people dressed in clothes of every color in very simple fabrics of wool or linen, merchants hawking their wares, the smells of fresh food baking in the sun! I get strange looks from the townsfolk as I dart around Friar Tuck, sniffing the air as we walk deeper into the marketplace.

Not all of the smells are great, by the way. I'm pretty certain they haven't invented indoor bathrooms yet.

The merchants wave at us, trying to get us to buy things. Friar Tuck shakes his head cheerfully, occasionally tossing out a coin. He keeps stealing glances at me, an amused smile on his face, like he's watching a little kid exploring the world for the first time. In a way, he is! I may not be little, but this world is certainly new, and full of wonder. He hasn't asked me any personal questions, like why Robin and I were in the forest, or where we came from. He'd never guess the truth of it.

I'm drawn toward a stall filled with fish swimming in a bucket. Real live fish! And some not-so-alive ones on wooden slabs. I stick my face down low to look at them up close, then wrinkle my nose at the smell and move on quickly. The next stall has a sign that reads *SPICE IT UP*, filled with powdered food with cool-sounding names like cloves and ginger and oats, wheat, barley, and sugar.

"Plum pie!" a heavyset lady calls out as she fans herself with her hand.

"Ribs of beef!" shouts a bald man with a golden hoop in his ear. Eggs and apples and candlesticks and corn. I can't believe the earth provides all these things. The people at home would never believe a place like this exists. I'm having a hard time believing it myself.

I wish Robin were here to share it. I hope he understands why I needed to go with Friar Tuck. It's only the second time in my life I've gotten to make my own choice — the first being just yesterday, when I decided to go after King Richard. I guess that first choice didn't turn out so well. Best not think about that, though.

"Are you thirsty?" the friar asks me.

"A little," I admit, although truthfully I'm absolutely parched. At home the medi-bots ensure we always stay hydrated. I'm going to have to look after my own bodily needs now. How strange! "But I fear I've already made you late enough for the meditation hour."

"Nonsense," he says, turning into the nearest tavern. "There's always time for a drink."

The air inside the Three Moons Tavern is cooler than outside, and with only the front window to let in some sunlight, it is quite dark. A quick glance around at the candles and oil lamps confirms the lack of electricity on this planet.

The door bangs closed and the man behind the bar squints out at us. He gives Friar Tuck a wave and finishes wiping out a glass with a rag. He has two fingers missing on his left hand. I try not to stare, but I doubt I'm doing a good job. I've never seen anyone whose body did not heal itself.

"You're coming next week, ain't ya?" the barman asks with a lopsided grin. His teeth could use a good brushing, but who am I to say so? I haven't brushed mine in two days.

"Indeed I am," the friar replies. "Haven't missed a chance to judge the sheriff's archery contest in ten years."

"Good to hear it," the barman says with a satisfied nod. "You're the only honest judge in the bunch."

"It's the sheriff I have to keep honest," Friar Tuck replies in a low voice. Then he orders himself a large glass of ale and adds, "And my newest student here will have your finest wine." Then he thinks better of it. "Make that water. And be sure to clean out the glass this time."

But instead of water, the bartender hands me a chipped mug full of an orange liquid. "Pumpkin cider," he says. "House specialty." Steam rises from the top of the mug, and my hands feel warm holding it. I take a sip and instantly scald the roof of my mouth.

"Delicious!" I declare, trying not to show how much pain I'm in as I take big, gulping breaths. The drink tastes sweeter than the little blue fruit balls, if that's possible. I manage to scald myself only a little bit less on the second sip. Friar Tuck shakes his head. "Didn't your mother teach you to wait for your drink to cool?"

I shake my head. "Actually, no." I don't tell him it's because I've never tasted anything hot before.

"Marrying off this young lady to an old coot, too?" a man hunched over the end of the bar suddenly asks. In the gloom, I hadn't noticed him there. He steps forward, and I can see he is about twenty years old, dressed in colorful clothes and scarves and holding an instrument of some sort. He strums the strings and music fills the small room.

He bows his head in my direction. "Alan-a-Dale, wandering minstrel, at your service. You may call me Alan." Then he turns to Friar Tuck, purses his lips, and gives him a hard stare.

Friar Tuck holds up his hand. "It is my duty to perform Lady Elly's wedding, Alan. I am sorry her marrying causes you pain." He pats the man gently on the shoulder.

Alan strums a melancholy tune and sighs. "'Tis wrong of me to blame you for doing your job. But we are in love. She does not love Sir Stephen — I'm certain of it."

Friar Tuck shakes his head. "I'm afraid love has very little to do with marriage."

Alan scoffs and turns back to me. "You don't believe that, do you, young lady? A girl's heart should be won with poetry and song and not given away to the highest bidder, no?"

His question takes me aback. I'm entirely unused to people asking me my thoughts on any subject, let alone a grown-up question like this. I decide to be honest. "Well, back home we do not marry for love, either." I don't add that I'm not even certain what romantic love is supposed to feel like.

He frowns. "That saddens me greatly. From where do you hail?"

I feel my cheeks grow hot as Friar Tuck also pauses in his drink for my answer. "It's far from here, and, um, very different. A city, actually."

I'm spared further questions by the door banging open. A hulking man dressed all in black steps inside — and all talking in the pub instantly halts. Instead of a hat or hood, the head of a skinned animal sits on the man's head. For a split second I worry it's Deedee, but this animal is darker and furrier. *Was* darker and furrier.

My stomach churns just the same.

Friar Tuck reaches out one arm and pushes me behind him. Alan steps forward, and together they hide me from view. The man grunts as he stomps past us, and my nose wrinkles at the dank smell that rises off him.

"Pint of ale!" he barks at the barman. "Now!"

"Sir Guy Gisborne," Alan whispers as they shuffle me out the door, still hidden. "The sheriff's number one henchman."

"What's a henchman?" I ask.

"A bad man doing the bidding of a worse one," Friar Tuck answers. Once we're back in the busy marketplace and have left the pub behind, his face relaxes again. "Where are you staying these days?" Friar Tuck asks Alan. "I know your family worries."

"I am keeping safe," he insists. "I have good people around me, and we take care of each other. Although I confess I am not the best company these days." He holds up his instrument. "Still, a man with a harp is always welcome at the table."

"Then we will be on our way," the friar says. "Safe travels on your path."

"To you as well," Alan says with a nod. To me he adds, "Do not give up on romance, young miss. I know I won't." Then he rests his harp on his chest and strums the strings as he walks off toward the forest.

Friar Tuck sighs and shakes his head. "Musicians." Then he points in the opposite direction of the forest, where I can see the roofs of low buildings tucked into the hillside. "We go that way," he says. "To the School of the Perpetual Now."

"The School of the what now?" I ask.

"The Perpetual Now," he repeats. "We aim to live in the moment. Our modern lives are so busy, as I'm sure you know. We must learn to be where we are, at every moment. We do not worry about the future or dwell in the past. When our students finish their studies and go out in the world, they spread the message by example."

I have to strain hard not to let my jaw fall open. He thinks his world is modern and busy? He has no idea. All I can do is nod politely. "I appreciate all that you're doing for me," I tell him as we leave the town square behind, "but I don't have anything to pay you."

"Don't fret about that for now," he says. "We'll work something out with your family once you're settled. I'm sure they will want to know you're safe and not wandering through the forest."

I open my mouth to tell him that he will find no family here when my eye catches the suitcase he's been carrying for me since we left the forest. The suitcase with only one item of value in it now. Even though Grandmother can no longer speak, I think she'd be proud of me for what I'm doing. At least, I hope so. Pushing past the lump in my throat, I say, "Actually, I do have something I can pay you with. It's in the suitcase."

We stop on a dusty footpath that climbs into the hills for a rest. Friar Tuck lays the dented suitcase down on a flat rock. I give him a nod, and he swings it open. Grandmother's headpiece glitters in the sunlight. Friar Tuck lifts it out and turns it around in his hands. He tucks it into his robes. "This will be more than sufficient."

I feel a flash of panic that I just gave away my only bargaining tool in this new world. But Father always said never to be indebted to anyone for anything if you can help it. Now I am officially a student, albeit one without any way to pay for anything.

As the friar clicks the suitcase closed, I spot a tiny white marble and recognize it as the pearl on the necklace Robin stuffed in there. The rest had rolled underneath my old clothes. I have not given away my last item of worth after all. The knot in my throat loosens, and I mouth a silent *thank you* to Robin, wherever he is.

As we resume our walk up the winding path, Friar Tuck begins telling me the history of the school. Then he pauses at the sound of footfalls above us. My first thought is that somehow the men from the forest have found us — but no, of course they wouldn't be here. Bounding down the hillside toward us is a pretty girl in brown pants and a red tunic. Her dark braid swings behind her.

"Was that Alan-a-Dale you were just talking to?" she asks Friar Tuck breathlessly when she reaches us. "He's soooo handsome." Her eyes get all soft and, well, *gooey*. "And he plays so beautifully." She turns to me, waiting for me to agree, I suppose. "Um, he's okay, I guess?" is the best I can offer.

A flash of surprise crosses her face as she no doubt realizes I'm not someone she knows. "Oh, I'm sorry, we haven't met. I'm Kylea, Friar Tuck's favorite student." She laughs and holds out her hand. She reminds me a little of Sarena, but perhaps that's only because not many girls my age ever speak to me.

"I'm Marian," I say, grasping her hand and shaking it. "Friar Tuck's *newest* student."

Kylea links her arm through mine. "Your voice sounds like a song! We shall be fast friends, I know it!" I can't help but notice the bracelet of multicolored beads curled around her arm. She sees me looking and says, "These are mala beads. They help me meditate better. I'll show you how to make your own in crafts class." I can't imagine owning anything that colorful, let alone wearing it on my body. I squeeze her arm with pleasure.

Friar Tuck chuckles. "You'll need to get to know each other quickly, girls. You know what happens when we arrive at school."

"What happens?" I ask, feeling my first trickle of worry. What have I signed up for?

The concern must have come through in my voice, because Kylea squeezes my arm. "It's nothing bad, truly. The students just don't talk. We're in silent retreat on school grounds this month."

Friar Tuck nods. "It is easiest to listen to the world around you when all you hear is the voice in your head. And when you turn that off, too? The silence will be like the loudest, purest music you've ever heard. You are at peace, in harmony with the present moment — the never-ending Perpetual Now."

I have a hard time picturing Kylea silent, but the friar's words stir up the same longing in me as when he first spoke of the school.

We travel a few more yards up the path, with Kylea chattering about the dormitory where we'll live, how the friars sometimes start to spontaneously dance, and which foods to avoid at meals, when a strong breeze carries the sound of cheering and the clanging of metal up to us. I stop and turn back to the village below, trying to determine where it's coming from.

The others stop, too. "Oh, that's just the outlaws and

vagabonds who live in Sherwood Forest," Kylea says, waving a hand dismissively. "They've offended the Sheriff of Nottingham one way or another, so they hide out and cause trouble in the woods. They never come into the village, though, because they don't want the sheriff's men to spot them. And don't worry — they never, ever come all the way to the school. We're hidden away, like a secret."

That's not what I'm worried about. I glance at Friar Tuck. He puts a reassuring hand on my shoulder. "I'm certain your friend is fine," he says. "He is no doubt far away from there by now."

I nod. I'm sure he's right. Robin is a fast runner. He's probably found another town on the other side of the forest and is right now tasting the local fare like I did. Maybe he even has a lead on parts to repair our airship by now, or at least to fix the hole in the hull. Yes, I'm sure he's left those men in his dust.

I link my arm back through Kylea's.

"So, what were you saying about the turnip soup?" I ask.

CHAPTER SEVENTEEN

↞ Robin ↠

I have just enough time to duck out of sight behind a tree before four boots burst onto the path, kicking up dirt. The rest of the men can't be far behind.

"The noise came from here," one says. "It must still be nearby."

It? Now that's insulting.

"You're lucky you have such bad aim," the other man says. I breathe a sigh of relief. I may be an "it," but at least I won't be shot with an arrow. Then he adds, "You know how attached the sheriff is to his deer."

Wait, what? I risk taking a glance. Two uniformed men stand beneath a tree, one holding a tube to his eye to scan the area. These men in brown uniforms aren't the ones we encountered by the stream. And I'm not their prey, nor is Marian or Friar Tuck. *Deedee* is! These must have been the men shooting into the trees. I look around and spot Deedee's nose sticking out from behind a wide tree. Neither man is looking her way. Guess I'm going to have to start making some noise again to distract them.

I step out onto the dirt, loudly crunching leaves underfoot as I go. The men's heads whirl around. "Who goes there?" the taller of the two demands.

"It is I, Robin Hood of Locksley." I bow as gracefully as

I can — which, I discover, I'm actually quite good at. "But you can call me Robin."

"I have never seen you before," the other says with narrowed eyes. The sun glints off the star-shaped badges on their chests. *Sheriff's Deputy.* That sounds important. "I know everyone within a hundred miles of here. What business have you in Sherwood Forest?" he demands.

I can't very well tell them that my airship from a spaceport many light-years away crash-landed here and now I'm trying to get us home. So I repeat what I told the other people we met on this planet. "Merely passing through, deputies. I'll get out of your way now." I tip my hat at them, willing Deedee to stay in place.

"Wait," the taller guy says as I begin to turn away.

I knew it wouldn't be that easy. I stop, prepared to be grabbed by the arm.

But all he does is ask, "Have you seen a small deer? Spots down his back and whatnot? We have to account for every last fawn or the sheriff gets grouchy. You don't want to be around the sheriff when he's grouchy."

"No, sir, you do not," the other deputy agrees. "Did you see it come this way?"

"Nope." This is not a lie. I did not see Deedee come this way. They aren't asking if I see her now, out of the corner of my eye, chewing a blade of grass. Which I do.

"This is a fool's errand," the tall deputy scoffs. "Let's get back to the castle." To me he says, "I wouldn't linger in these woods past dark. Not safe for a stranger when outlaws have moved in. We just chased off a group of thieves now."

He reaches into a bag and I gasp as he holds up my two small statues — the bird and the round-bellied man. "Found these things on the scoundrels! Bet the sheriff will forget all about the deer when we give him these. Not much to look at, but they should be worth a whole bunch of shillings."

I start to sputter something like, *Wha — That's my — How did you —* then make myself stop. The statues must have fallen from the pockets of my cloak when I was shooting. But if I try to claim them, these men will never believe I hadn't stolen them in the first place.

The deputies don't waste another minute on me. The man with my statues sticks two fingers into his mouth. A shrill whistle blasts the air between us, and a few seconds later two enormous creatures trot onto the path. They have to duck under the branches in order to fit!

I jump backward, smacking my back against a tree. The creatures stand beside the men, and I'm amazed that their thin, spindly legs can hold up their huge bodies and long necks.

The deputies swing their legs over the animals' bodies and reach for the pieces of rope hanging on either side of the long, thick necks. Then the deputies dig in their heels, give a one-word command, and the animals carry them away. As the dust and leaves settle back down, the name comes to me. "Horses!" I shout to no one.

How I wish Marian could have been here to see them! Did I make the wrong choice to let her go? I don't have a single thing to barter with now — just my charm, and that's running pretty thin. What good is going into town with nothing to sell or barter? My stomach is rumbling, though, and I'm thirsty. The extra food rations I packed are lost in the void of space.

With Deedee at my side, I make my way back through the woods in the direction of the stream. I decide to approach it from much farther down, though, in case the deputies didn't chase the outlaws away as well as they thought.

The water is just as crisp and refreshing as it was this morning, although having a deer as a drinking companion is not as much fun as having a person. Marian, specifically.

The stream is much wider and deeper at this end, with fallen trees making bridges across it every few yards. I entertain myself by running back and forth across them, not slipping once. Deedee puts one hoof on the log, but thinks better of it and watches from the shore.

"Think I can do it with my eyes closed?" I ask Deedee. "Let's find out." I slip off my shoes, relishing the feel of the bark beneath my feet as I inch forward. It's slippery, but that makes it more of a challenge.

I'm already halfway across the stream when Deedee makes one of her bleeting noises. "Don't worry," I call over my shoulder. "I'm not going to fall." I'm about to lift my right foot when a voice replies, "Oh, I'm not worried. This is very entertaining."

My eyes fly open and I whirl around, feet sliding in all directions. I fall right on my butt and wince at the pain. Instinctively my arms grab for the log and only my feet wind up in the cold, rushing water.

It takes longer than it should for me to recognize that what I'm looking at is a man, and not a tree. He is twice the width of any man I've seen on this planet so far, and half again as tall.

His voice rumbles down at me. "You are trespassing on my bridge."

"I didn't realize the forest belonged to anyone," I manage to say.

The man shrugs. "Nevertheless. Guess we'll have to fight for it now." He holds up what I assume at first to be a long branch. But then he flips it around in his hands and I see it's more polished than that, with steel at both ends. It's a weapon.

I scramble off the log to the opposite side of the stream. "No need," I call across to him. "The bridge is all yours."

But he shakes his head. "Are you afraid to fight me?"

Yes. But I can't let him know that. I square my shoulders and put on my best fake-it-till-you-make-it voice. "Robin Hood is afraid of no one."

"Then bring your quarterstaff and prove it."

I don't own a quarterstaff, nor do I know what one is. I'm about to tell him this, but he's already stepping onto the log bridge, swinging his weapon back and forth over his head. I'm surprised the log can hold his weight, but I don't have too long to marvel at it. I scan the ground until I find a fallen branch. It will have to do. I imitate the positioning of his hands — one in the center of the branch, and one midway to the top.

Too quickly he reaches my side of the shore and is upon me, his first blow leaving a long scrape down my arm. I feel the sting and catch sight of blood out of the corner of my eye. My first thought is that I must take a trip to the nurse for healing. My second thought is how crazy my first thought was.

Summoning my old fencing skills, I come out swinging. I lunge, he parries, and my branch hits air. Then he lunges to the left, and I block the blow by raising my branch to meet his staff with a split second to spare. His face registers surprise; then he breaks into a smile and says, "And here I was thinking this wouldn't be a fair fight."

We continue to swing and thrust, each of us getting in the occasional hit against the other. I quickly realize the quarterstaff is different than fencing, and have to adjust my moves to counter his. He is much bigger, but I am faster and have youth on my side. He backs me up to the edge of the stream, and I have no choice but to hop onto the nearest log bridge or wind up in the water.

I fight him off as I scramble backward on the log, slipping and regaining my balance over and over. I'm quickly tiring, but trying not to show it. It feels like we've been at this forever, but in truth it probably hasn't even been ten minutes.

And now he's on the log with me! "Is that a deer?" he shouts, and when I'm stupid enough to turn my head, he swings his staff in front of him and sweeps my feet right off the log. The rest of my body follows, sailing through the air and landing facedown in the icy water.

The water is refreshing when you're drinking it. Not so much when you're submerged in it and don't know how to swim. The only body of water I've ever been in is a bathtub, and this ain't that.

Two huge hands grab under my armpits and lift me straight out of the water like I don't weigh more than a leaf. He drops me, sputtering, onto the shore. I watch as my staff/branch drifts downstream, well out of reach. I close my eyes and wait for the final blow to come.

"John Little is the name," the man booms. "Glad to have such a worthy opponent. No one's ever lasted that long before."

I allow myself to peek up at him, and see that he's smiling! I scramble to my feet and shake the hand he's holding out. "John Little?" I repeat. "Your name should be Little John instead. You know, to be funny. Because you're enormous."

He throws his head back with a deep laugh. "I like it! From now on, I'm Little John." He leans over, fishes my soaking-wet hat out of the water, and plops it on my head.

The feather hangs limply over my ear. I push it back and smooth it into place.

"Sorry about using your bridge," I tell him. "I'll be on my way."

"Where you headed?" he asks.

I have no idea doesn't sound like a good enough answer. So I don't say anything.

"You live nearby?" he asks.

I shake my head.

"Got any money?"

I shake my head again. "I had some items of value, but the sheriff's deputies took them."

He grimaces. "You will have to pay double their worth to get them back."

"I'd need a job first."

"You got any talents? You're good with the staff, so that's something."

"I can fence," I tell him. "And shoot arrows. I can juggle fire sticks without setting anything on fire. Usually."

He appraises me, then says, "We have fencers and archers, and every jester can juggle. What else you got?"

Is getting in trouble a lot a talent? "Um, I can make things disappear," I say, scooping up a pebble from the edge of the stream. I hold it up with my right hand, pretend to place it in my left, and close that hand tight. While he's looking there, I use my right thumb to push the pebble between two fingers of my right hand until it's sticking out the back toward me. Then I hold both hands palm up to show they're empty. His eyes widen with delight, and he clasps me on the shoulder with his big hand.

"Good enough! You'll come with me. The boys can always use some entertaining. It's a hard life, hiding out in the woods. And don't get me wrong, but you don't look like you've spent much time outdoors."

Can't argue with that. "I appreciate the offer, but are you an . . . outlaw?" I don't have much interest in spending any more time with the group I met earlier.

"We don't like that word," Little John replies. "Makes it sound like we did something wrong. It's the sheriff's rules that are impossible to live by. You chop down a tree for wood to heat your home and the sheriff brands you a thief and takes your house. You shoot a deer to feed your family? He tosses you in jail. He thinks he owns these whole woods. No one can own the woods."

"Um, don't you own that bridge?"

He chuckles. "Nah. Just felt like a good fight."

I shake my head. "Hope I gave you one."

He rubs a purple bump forming on his arm and grimaces. "That you did. So you coming or not?"

I nod. I don't think I'll be getting a better offer today.

He leads me away from the stream, away from where the ship landed, toward a part of the forest I haven't seen before. The trees and grasses are much denser here, with no path to help me keep my bearings. We march on in silence for a long time. Then he says, "Anything else you want to tell me? Besides why you're wearing all green. You look like an overgrown clump of grass."

I let the insult pass. "What do you want to know?"

He gestures behind us with his thumb without stopping his march. "You can tell me why one of the sheriff's deer has been following us since we left the stream."

"You're not going to trick me with that twice," I say innocently.

He rolls his eyes but doesn't ask again.

"Home away from home," he finally announces, pushing aside heavy branches and gesturing around us. I hear the loud clanging of metal before I see anyone. Little John makes a wide berth around two groups of men practicing sword fighting, and we step into a clearing, where tents and lean-tos and even some mud houses crowd between the trees. Men of all shapes and sizes are busy sharpening weapons, stirring pots over fires, eating, drinking, and singing.

Singing?

"Attention, everyone!" Little John calls out. "We've got a new member of the gang. He's brave enough to fight me, he's quick, and he can make things disappear. I give you Robin Hat!"

"Er, Hood," I correct him as the sword fights halt and the group shouts their welcomes. "Not Hat." As silly as Hood sounds, it's the name Marian gave me, and that means something.

"Oops, sorry, men," Little John says. "That's Hood, Robin *Hood*."

A few men wave and others nod at me. Then they start belting out their rowdy tune again. I turn to my new friend. "For outlaws they're certainly a merry bunch of men."

Little John turns back to the crowd. "Robin Hood here just christened you the Merry Men!" he shouts. "And you all may call me Little John now!"

The men cheer, "Long live Little John and Robin Hood and the Merry Men!" and break into another song. They really *are* merry.

I scan the crowd and am relieved when I only recognize one person from the group Marian and I encountered earlier. It is the man with the yellow hair, the one the leader had suggested be Marian's groom. Thankfully he had been the least obnoxious of the bunch.

He recognizes me and dashes over. "I apologize for my companions' poor treatment of you and your maiden earlier," he says, grasping my hand. "My cousin and his friends can be crude, but they took me in when I didn't have anyone else." He keeps shaking my hand, up and down, up and down. "The name is Much, the miller's son."

"Much?" I repeat.

"Yessir. My father — may he rest in peace — gave me that name because he said I had as much energy as five kids."

Suddenly *Hood* doesn't seem as odd. "Well, Much, it's nice to meet you."

"Let poor Robin eat," Little John says, tugging me toward the closest fire pit. "Can't you see he's wasting away?"

Well, I don't know about *that*. Everyone's skinny where I come from. Our food squares don't allow us to store up much fat. My stomach growls loudly, which makes Little John and Much laugh. "Do you guys do this often? Pick up strangers on the street and share your food with them?"

They shake their heads. "We avoid everyone who crosses the Great North Road through the forest whenever possible," Much says. "You can't be too careful these days. People can be more dangerous than they look."

"But you approached me," I remind Little John. "What if *I'm* more dangerous than I look?"

He makes a show of looking me up and down. "Nah. You're *less* dangerous than you look."

I'm about to argue that he hasn't seen me with a bow and arrow, but I've just been handed some kind of food wrapped up in some other kind of food and it smells delicious. All other thoughts vanish.

I eat until my stomach groans. "What is this called?" I ask Much, wiping my mouth with the back of my hand.

Much shrugs. "We're not picky here. It's a stew made out of yesterday's dinner."

"Well, what was yesterday's dinner?"

He shrugs again. "A stew made from the day before's dinner!"

I see I'm not going to get anywhere, so I just pat my belly. "Delicious! You could charge a fortune for this!"

Little John laughs. "You must not be too picky either."

A new arrival steps into the clearing. "Minstrel! Play us a tune!" the group shouts.

But the young man, garbed in scarves of orange, yellow, and blue, shakes his head and sets down his instrument. "I am too heartbroken to play."

Little John nods knowingly. "This is Alan-a-Dale, the finest minstrel in the whole county of Nottingham."

Does anyone here have a normal name?

"He taught us every song we know," Much adds. "He's usually very cheery."

Alan plops down on the log beside me and puts his face in his hands.

"His true love is marrying another a few days hence," Much explains. "A wealthy old bore with boils on his nose."

"Ouch."

"Elly and I are in love," Alan says with a sigh. "But it would take more money than I could make in five years to compete with the man her greedy father has chosen for her."

He launches into a love song about two hearts bound together that, before I met Marian, would probably have made me want to gag. But now . . . it's kinda nice. And sad. And I find myself swept along with his voice like everyone else.

Then, before I can stop myself, I jump up from the log and announce, "The wedding must be stopped!"

Alan doesn't even look up from his instrument. "And who's going to stop it?"

"I will!" I declare — then instantly want to bite my tongue.

Now he looks up and seems to really notice me for the first time. "And you are?"

"He's Robin Hood!" Much says. "The bravest of the brave! The most clever, daring, charming outlaw in Sherwood Forest, nay, all of Nottingham!"

The men all begin to chant, "Robin! Robin! Robin!"

Hmm, not sure about all those things he said, but I stand a little taller.

"You must have a lost love you need to win back, too!" Alan says, his eyes glittering now with excitement. "For you to understand so well."

"Of course he does!" Much shouts. Then he lowers his voice. "Do you?"

"I do!" I hear myself say. I mean, I am trying to get Marian back home safely, so that counts, right? And just like Alan, I'll need money to do it.

"What is your plan?" Little John asks me when the cheers die down.

I take a minute to answer. Then half to myself I mumble, "If Shane were here he'd come up with something."

"Shall we go find this Shane person?" Little John asks, rising from the log.

I pull him back down. "No, he's very far away."

"I have long legs," Little John says. "I can walk quickly."

"Trust me, it's farther than your legs could ever carry you." My mind runs through some of my exploits back on

Delta Z, but tricking little kids into giving up their tokens probably won't work here. But maybe something else will — like Shane's con with the card game! *First let them play, then make them pay.* An idea starts to form.

"What if we find rich people on the road who are tired and hungry from travel — and offer them a meal and some entertainment?" I ask. "Then at the end, we tell them to pay for it?"

Little John considers this. "And if they won't pay?"

"Well then, we can let them barter something of worth that we can sell later. Or challenge them to a quarterstaff fight with you, or an archery match with me. And when they lose — and they *will* lose — they'll have no choice but to pay up."

"You're that good?" he asks.

"I am."

"It's pretty sneaky," Little John says uncertainly. "But it's for love, right?"

The men gathered around start cheering, "Do it for love! Do it for love!"

I look at Alan. He nods. "Yes," I reply. "It's for love." A tiny gnawing feeling in my stomach tells me that Marian would not approve of my methods any more than she had of Shane's, but I push that aside. A man's gotta do what a man's gotta do.

CHAPTER EIGHTEEN

Marian

It's been a week since I arrived at the School of the Perpetual Now. At first my belly had a constant ache from all the strange new foods and drinks, but as long as I don't stuff myself, I'm usually okay. I miss some of the comforts of home, but a vita-square definitely isn't one of them.

I've already learned more here than in ten years of school in The City, and I've made friends — friends who don't have to be nice to me just because of who my parents are. Even though we can't speak to one another with words, it's amazing how much you can communicate with facial expressions. Kylea is a whiz at the eye roll, and I'm a natural at wide-eyed wonder, since it's what I feel all the time. The pledge of silence has relieved me of answering questions about my past, which is a relief. It's not like I could tell *that* story with just my face!

The school's library has become my second home. I wander through the shelves for hours at a time, trailing my fingertips along the books' spines, mesmerized by all the knowledge and stories they contain. I even tried putting one on my head once and walking with it. Forget improving my posture — that thing was heavy! Perhaps my teacher had been wrong about that historical practice. Plus, I got strange looks.

When I'm not reading out in the garden or watching the friars dance on the lawn, I'm standing over the scribes' desks, watching them transform blank paper into words and drawings. They call their "paper" *vellum*, and it's made from animal skin, a fact I'm trying very hard to ignore. I want to tell the scribes that they can make paper out of trees or rocks, but that pesky pledge of silence keeps me mute. No doubt the scribes are grateful for that pledge, because without it I'd be badgering them with questions all day.

I watch in awe as they color in the letters and paint tiny pictures around the margins of the pages with even tinier brushes. Kylea promised to show me how to make different color paints for them out of crushed fruits, flowers, and eggs. She's been very kind to me. I am very glad she was assigned as my roommate, even though last night her snores were as loud as an airship coming in for a landing.

My hands haven't gotten that numb, anxious feeling all week.

"Ready?" Friar Tuck asks, putting his hand on my shoulder. I nod and step away from the scribe. I'm fairly certain I hear the scribe give a sigh of relief.

Today is my first private meditation session, and I'm a little nervous, but it's a manageable nervous. I've watched the daily meditation hour each day from the front lawn, but I couldn't hear the instructions. Everyone seems so happy and calm after. Starting mediation is the only thing that would make me want to leave the warm, cozy embrace of the library.

Well, that and mealtime. I probably shouldn't have had that extra helping (okay, two helpings) of blackberry pie at dinner last night. My stomach is churning a bit as I follow Friar Tuck out to the garden where the classes are held.

"The first thing we're going to do is teach you how to eat correctly," he says.

Uh-oh! Have I been eating wrong? I feel my cheeks get hot.

He leads me over to a small table where a slice of orange, a lump of meat, and a cup of tea lie on a tin plate. "Have you noticed you eat a bit . . . differently from the others at your table?"

I open my mouth to answer, then remember the pledge of silence and shake my head instead. But if I have to be fully honest, I haven't really been looking up from my plate enough to notice how others are eating. Those etiquette classes at home didn't cover mealtimes. Why would they when all we eat are vita-squares?

"I've watched you," he says, pulling a stool out for me from under the table. "You eat like it's a competition. You need to learn to savor your food, to be fully present in the act of nourishing your body. You want to eat each meal like it's your first."

How can I explain that each meal practically IS my first? He instructs me on how to chew the orange slice slowly, to feel the sweetness on my tongue, to silently thank the orange tree that grew it so that I could enjoy its juice. That's a lot to remember while eating an orange!

But I do as he says, and find that it actually elevates the experience to a whole new level of wonderfulness (and messiness). I'm sure my juice-filled smile is letting the friar know that. If I ever get back home, the first thing I'm going to do is show Grandmother how to eat an orange.

"Excellent," he says when I lay down the peel. "Now try the hare." He points to the lump of meat. I pick it up in my hands and bring it toward my mouth.

"Thank the rabbit for giving its life to nourish yours, and then — Is everything all right, child?"

He is looking at me with concern. My expression must mirror the horror I am feeling. A hare is a rabbit? And a rabbit is a bunny! The school has served this same meal at least three times since I've been here, and other meats, as well. I've been eating ANIMALS? I've been eating BUNNIES? I drop the food back down to my plate and start to cry. How could I not have understood this?

He dismisses me for the day. At dinner I am served a thick slice of brown bread and a stew made of cabbage and carrots. I almost cry again out of relief. I eat the stew slowly and savor every bite.

"Ready for your next lesson?" Friar Tuck asks the next morning. I nod, eager to put yesterday behind me. We head to the garden again, but this time we keep going, all the way to a path lined with bushes and flowers. I've seen people walking on it, but have no idea where it leads. Now I see it's just a wide circle around the school and the barn. "We're going to start with a walking meditation. What we learn from it is at the core of what we work toward at the school."

I give a thumbs-up and close my eyes, ready to start. He laughs. "You cannot move along the path with your eyes closed. You'll walk right into a bramble bush."

Right! I open them and smile sheepishly. In the meditation hour, everyone has their eyes closed. But of course they're seated on the lawn. Friar Tuck begins to walk, and I quickly follow.

"For the first circle, you will try to focus your attention on every flower, every leaf, every shadow cast onto the ground, for these will look different tomorrow. This exact moment will never come again, and we are lucky enough to witness it." He waits to see if I'm following, so I give a quick nod.

He continues. "Like an anchor connects a boat to the sea, when we meditate, our breath connects our awareness and our inner thoughts to our body. In a walking meditation, our feet do that for us. As they connect with the ground, they remind us to focus our attention inward. We use this movement of our bodies to remind ourselves that we are here, at this moment."

He gestures around him with his arms, and waits for me to do the same. I giggle. This isn't like any class I've ever had.

"By learning to switch our awareness from our outer world to our inner world and back again," he says, ignoring my little interruption, "we learn to gain control over our thoughts. We learn to make better decisions when we can retreat inward to think, without the distractions of the world around us. Then we are also able to step out of our heads, and be at one with the world's bounty — the people and nature that surrounds us, which we might otherwise take for granted."

I nod excitedly. I'm bursting to tell him that I've been doing the walking meditation since I've gotten here, without realizing it. I don't take any of nature for granted — how could I? It's all brand-new to me. And the silent retreat has lifted the burdens of saying what I know people want to hear — something my mother and teachers have been grooming me to do since birth. I feel tears sting my eyes and quickly wipe at them.

Friar Tuck puts his hand on my shoulder. "Why don't you accompany Kylea into town today for her weekly journey? She's our best shopper. You could use the break, I think."

I smile, wanting to appear grateful, although truly I've already shopped enough for two lifetimes. Still, when Kylea finds me after lunch and loops her arm through mine, I feel my excitement bubble up. I enjoyed the solitude that being alone with my thoughts had afforded me, but it will be nice to talk for a change.

Kylea doesn't waste a single moment. As soon as we begin our descent down the steep hillside, a rush of words pours out of her. She asks how I like school, the grounds, the teachers, the books, the food, the clothes, and does she really snore?

I laugh, and my voice sounds unfamiliar to me at first when I answer her questions. Is it really as high-pitched as that? As we approach the village, I begin to tune her out and practice the part of the walking mediation where I focus on what's around me — the brightly colored leaves, the crunch of the pebbles underfoot, the smells wafting to us from below, the energy of the shoppers in the marketplace. In the distance I can hear a harp and wonder if it's that man with the odd name, the one whose true love is marrying another.

We're almost run over by a group of boys and girls weaving in and out of the stalls singing "He robs from the rich, from the rich, from the rich, and he gives to the poor, yes, he gives to the poor. He's a hero!" They weave and sing, over and over. I stop to watch them, humming along to the catchy tune. I've never seen kids sing with such abandon. Things like that just aren't done in The City. I have to run to catch up to Kylea, who is haggling with a merchant over the price of a bag of beans.

The singing stops abruptly, and when I turn to see why, my mouth drops open. A man with short red hair riding an enormous brown animal comes bounding into the middle of the square. He climbs off the animal's back and pulls a scroll of some sort from a bag attached to the saddle. Shoppers begin streaming over from the stalls, leaving their purchases unpaid and the merchants scowling after them.

I grab on to Kylea. "What is THAT?"

"The sheriff's deputy?" she asks, following my shaking finger. "He's just posting the latest Wanted notice. Turning in an outlaw is an easy way to earn some gold."

"Not the *deputy*," I cry. "The beast!"

She laughs. "The horse?"

"Horses are *real*? I always though they were a myth!"

She tilts her head at me. "You truly are an odd one." Oh boy, she doesn't know the half of it.

The deputy finishes nailing up the paper and the crowd surges forward. Kylea pushes up to the front, but I hang back. I'm unable to take my eyes off the horse, who is now bending its long neck toward the ground to allow the man to climb back on. After being shot at by one outlaw and nearly married off to another, I'm not interested in whatever the poster says. If I spotted him I'd run in the opposite direction anyway.

The deputy digs his heels into the horse's sides. Dust flies up into the crowd as the animal takes off. I watch until they turn the corner, heading toward a part of the village I haven't seen before. Then Kylea lets out a loud whistle and announces, "Now *that's* one handsome boy! If I found him I might keep him for myself instead of turning him in!"

Two other women giggle. "Me, too!" one says. The other reads out, "'Wanted dead or alive by the Sheriff of Nottingham for thievery, sword fighting without a license, and general mischief. Goes by the names Robin Hat, Robin Hood, Robin of Locksley, and The Man in Green. Reward: one hundred gold coins.'"

I had been only half listening at first, but now my heart is slamming against my chest. I rush up to Kylea's side. The pencil sketch doesn't capture the green of his eyes, but the artist got the sly smile just right, and that silly hat with the feather. There's no doubt, it's . . .

"Robin?" a shocked male voice behind me exclaims. Then he dissolves into laughter and says, "Why am I not surprised?"

I whirl around, having no idea who I'm about to see.

He spots me at the same moment and breaks into a wide grin. "There you are, Marian! You're a hard girl to find! I have a message for you from your grandmother."

I'm having trouble processing the sight before me. In the middle of a medieval village, hundreds of light-years from where he's supposed to be, stands, impossibly, Robin's cousin, Will.

I gape at him, at an utter loss for words. Kylea finally tears herself away from the Wanted poster. Her eyebrows shoot up when she sees us. She hurries over, looking back and forth between us. I watch as her eyes takes in his pale never-seen-the-sun skin, his green clothes. "Is this boy bothering you, Marian?"

I shake my head slowly, keeping my eyes glued on Will's. How is he standing here?

But Will must have taken the same charm lessons Robin had. He flashes Kylea a wide grin, and I can't help notice his teeth are stained a light blue color. He bows slightly. "Will Stutely at your service, pretty lady."

Kylea actually blushes! "Any friend of Marian's is a friend of mine," she replies, sticking out her hand. Will reaches over and kisses the back of it! That's enough to break me out of my stupor.

I turn to Kylea and hold up one finger. "Be right back." She watches with a silly grin on her face as I grab Will by the shirt and drag him to the side of the marketplace.

"How?" I demand, figuring one word summed it up. I have to snap my fingers to get him to stop gazing past me at Kylea.

"This place is AMAZING!" he says, his deep brown eyes twinkling. "Trees! Fresh air! Birds! And the smells!" He inhales deeply, then wrinkles his nose. "Well, they're not all good. But wow! And have you tried those berries in the woods? I can't get enough of them!"

"I can tell that by your blue teeth. *Please* tell me what's going on so I don't think I'm hallucinating?"

He uses the collar of his shirt as a makeshift toothbrush, then pulls me into an alleyway between a tavern and a shop selling woven mats. "Okay, here goes. So of course the commander lost his mind when he realized Robin had taken the *Solar Hammer*, but Finley and I assured him the ship would be returned good as new in only a few days. But when the commander called down to the landing field on Earth, they swore that no ships had arrived from Delta Z. They said even if you'd landed in the Dead Zone, radar would have picked you up." Will pauses and waves his hands around. "I can see why you didn't want to come back, by the way, this place is —"

"The *Solar Hammer* crashed into pieces," I say bluntly.

"Oh." He lets his hands drop to his sides. "That's not good."

"Go on with your story," I urge.

"Okay. So then Elan tells me and Dad that he memorized the coordinates when he entered them. That kid is something. Did you know he can recite pi to hundreds of —"

"Will!"

"Sorry! So anyway, we couldn't find a ship to go look for you. Then my father and I got called into the command center. We had a video call from Earth! It was private, on a really high-level security channel, so even the commander had to leave. He was not happy, I can tell you that. Anyway, the call was from an old woman — your grandmother! She found out you hadn't gone to Earth Beta and said she was sending a ship to bring you home and —"

I hold up my hand. "Stop right there. My grandmother couldn't have called you. She can't speak."

He shrugs. "For someone who can't speak she sure had a lot to say. There's a tracker in the headpiece she gave you. It was set to activate when you landed on Earth Beta, and when it never did, she knew something was wrong."

I shake my head. "My grandmother doesn't *know* things. I mean, she's not all there, like, in the head."

"She's all there, all right," he says. "And then some. She was very bossy! After she got PJ to admit you'd stayed on Delta Z, she called my father. Apparently they know each other, from, like, years ago."

If my jaw wasn't already hanging open, it would have fallen open now.

"I know, weird, right?" he says. "So my dad had to tell her that you went off to try to find King Richard and that we hadn't heard from you since."

"What — what'd she say to that?" I ask, still finding it impossible to believe she could *say* anything.

"At first she laughed."

"She *laughed*?"

He nods. "She said she should have realized when you scaled a building instead of climbing the stairs on your mission to get the coordinates, and when you kept a copy, that she'd underestimated your bravery and dedication."

"My *grandmother* sent me on that mission? And she knew I kept the coordinates?"

"Yes," he says. "From what she was saying, she's been working for the resistance for years."

My grandmother has a *job*? "The resistance?" I repeat. "I've never heard of it."

"It's a group of people trying to get Prince John out of power." He puts his hand on my arm and squeezes reassuringly. "For what it's worth, your grandmother said she's very proud of you."

My head fills with flashes from that night — the strolling couple I kept running into, had they been in on it? And I'd run into Grandmother on the street! She seemed as out of it as always. But she wasn't, was she? She'd been distracting the guard! Why had she pretended all these years?

But I know the answer already. By pretending to not understand anything, no one considered her a threat. Officials would drop their guard around her. She must have heard all sorts of confidential information from Prince John and the other members of the government. Even her own son would have underestimated her! And then another thought — she must have been behind me getting picked for the trip to Earth Beta in the first place! Why couldn't she just have confided all this in me? Was Ivy in on it? My parents? Is that why my mother was so eager to have me go? But my father is loyal to Prince John. Isn't he?

Will has to snap his fingers in front of my face to bring my focus back. "You want to hear the rest?"

I blink a few times to clear my head. "Yes, of course, sorry!"

"Okay. So when the airship she sent arrived, instead of using it to send you home, we used it to get me here. To find you and Robin, and King Richard and —"

"But, Will, the coordinates were wrong, since they landed us all the way out here. The people on this planet have no idea about life on other planets. They couldn't possibly be involved with politics on a planet across the galaxy! They don't even know what a galaxy *is*!"

He smiles. "What better place to hide a king than the last place anyone would think to look?"

I blink hard. "Are you serious? You really think he's here? *Where?*"

"I have a good idea where he's being kept," he replies. "But first we need to find Robin. There's something really important that outlaw cousin of mine needs to know."

I wait for him to say more, but he doesn't. It finally hits me that the mission my grandmother sent me on? I'm still on it!

It takes another few seconds to register that Will's gone still, his gaze focused over my right shoulder. I slowly turn around to find Kylea standing a few feet behind me. Her arms are piled high with rolled-up straw mats that are slipping to the ground one by one. She doesn't seem to notice. I don't know how long she's been standing there, but obviously long enough to hear a lot of things she shouldn't have.

No doubt there's some sort of punishment for allowing

someone from a far less advanced civilization to overhear you talking about airships, space travel, and dead zones on ruined planets. I hold my breath, waiting to see if Kylea is going to faint or scream. I'm pretty sure those are the only two options in this situation.

For a long moment, her eyes flicker between the two of us. Then she lets out a deep breath and says, "So, which one of you is going to introduce me to Robin?"

Will recovers faster than I do. He bursts out laughing. I frown. Kylea drops the rest of her mats and links one arm through mine, just like she did when we first met. "Don't worry, Marian. I'm not really after Robin. Not when his dashing cousin is here." She pats Will on the arm. "But I *can* tell you where to find Sherwood's newest outlaw. We'll have to find some fancy clothes to change into first, though." She eyes Will up and down. "Is wearing all green a thing where you come from?"

"It is!" he says, beaming. "Do you like it?"

I don't wait for her to answer before saying, "Kylea, why do we need to dress up?"

She squeezes my arm, then links her other one through Will's. "Because we're going to a wedding tomorrow!"

CHAPTER NINETEEN

↢ Robin ↣

"Your teeth look too good," Much says as he looks me up and down. "How come you got such good teeth?"

He's right. My teeth stand out too much. Everyone on this planet has crooked, yellow, and/or missing teeth. I can't very well explain to Much about the excellent health care on Delta Z. They still stick leeches on people here when they're sick to "suck out the bad blood."

I dip my finger into the pile of cooled ashes from last night's fire and smear some on my front teeth. I already rubbed some across my chin and cheeks, exchanged my pointy hat for a plain brown wool cap that goes down low over my eyes, and tied back my hair. Combined with my plain new clothes (also known as Much's old clothes), my disguise is nearly complete. All I have to do is put a few pebbles in one shoe to change how I walk and no one will recognize me.

Needless to say, it's been a long week. It started off great. The Merry Men took me in, fed me, gave me a dry place to sleep, and let me show off my archery skills. I left one day to go check on the airship, careful to make sure no one followed me. This was accomplished by telling them I had a very upset stomach and needed to "go off into the woods to spend some time alone." No one asked any further questions.

The ol' *Solar Hammer 2000* was still there, looking even worse, as the weather had deposited leaves and other debris inside the giant hole. As I started to clean it out, my foot knocked against something hard, and I uncovered one of the swords my parents had left me!

I feel safer having a weapon at my side now. The Merry Men didn't even ask me where I got it. They're cool that way. My plan to invite rich people to dine with us only to ask for payment at the end has been working very well. Turns out no one wants to risk facing off with Little John, so they all empty their pockets without too much fuss. It isn't actually *stealing*; I mean, we give them a really good meal. Alan-a-Dale even sings for them, and I've been known to accurately name people's playing cards every single time (after secretly forcing their selection, of course!).

Flush with more money than the Merry Men had seen in a month, I took Alan into town a few days ago to get him a new outfit. If we're going to stop a wedding, he needs to look as good as possible to impress the bride and her family. On the way to the tailor, we passed an overcrowded orphanage with all these kids who didn't have any toys or warm blankets. It made me think of my parents and how I grew up without them but never wanted for anything. I will likely never get to see Uncle Kent or Will again, and they gave me so much. I'll never be able to repay them. But I could do something now, for these kids who don't have anyone looking after them.

So I emptied my pockets into their donation box. At first Alan wasn't thrilled with me for giving away all our money, but when he saw how happy the kids were, he came around. But it meant we had to start over. In my haste, I invited the wrong man to dinner. Sir Guy Gisborne. The man the sheriff hires to do his dirty work. Even the name makes me shudder.

We'd seen him traveling the road before. Little John had warned me to let him pass without stopping him, so I'd stayed hidden. But after I gave all our money away, I was feeling desperate, and I hadn't seen anyone else that day who looked wealthy enough to pay up.

Guy stopped by the side of the road so his horse could graze. As usual, he wore all black with a cape pulled over his head that looked like it was made from an animal skin — head and all. He was nearly as big as Little John, but much creepier.

"Good sir," I said, darting into the road in front of him. "You must be tired from your travels. I can offer you an excellent meal and fine company."

The man pushed back his hood and narrowed his eyes at me. Up close he smelled foul. He swiftly drew a sword from his belt and lunged almost before I had a chance to react. *Almost.* With inches to spare, I leapt off the road and landed on my back in the bushes. I sprang up and pulled out my own sword, saying a little prayer of thanks that I had worn it.

I came out swinging, but he definitely had the advantage. My fencing classes hadn't prepared me for fighting to the death with a man three times my size. And I was pretty sure that's what was happening.

We clashed and clanged our way from one side of the road to the other, both of us landing the occasional blow. It soon felt like no part of me had been left unbruised. And he'd sliced my shirt in three places! I desperately wished I'd brought some of the Merry Men with me as backup, but I'd proven to be the best at this first part of the plan. I had the innocence of youth on my side, and all that. Much would have come, but I'd convinced him he was too young. Now I'd have been grateful for anyone.

Finally, Guy swore and boomed, "Enough, boy! This is wasting my time. I am looking for a man named Robin Hood. An outlaw of the worst sort. Reportedly wears a silly brown hat with a red feather. You must know him."

"Why would you say that?" I asked, thankful for the fact that I'd forgotten my hat that morning in my haste.

He growled at me. "You tried to pull the same trick he's been doing this week. Luring people to dinner and then forcing them to pay. You should be more careful whose bad actions you try to imitate. Not everyone would be as understanding as me." He said this last part with a snarl.

"He doesn't *force* anyone to do anything," I insisted, then quickly added, "I mean, I'm sure he doesn't."

"Do you know him or not?" he demanded.

I shook my head as backup finally arrived in the form of Much, who jumped out onto the road and said the exact wrong thing at the wrong time. "There you are, Robin. We were getting —" He clamped his mouth shut when he saw the company I was keeping. But the damage had been done. I'll never forget the purple shade of Guy's face.

Thinking fast, I darted over and sliced through the rope Guy had used to tie his horse to a tree. "Your horse is getting away!" I shouted at him. And then Much and I ran faster in the other direction than we've ever run before. Neither of us got much sleep, fearing Guy or the sheriff's deputies would be out looking for us. Fortunately, the night passed without trouble.

"Are you sure he won't recognize me?" I ask Much now.

Much shakes his head. "He's looking for a young,

handsome man in green. And now you're, well, not that. He's probably forgotten all about you by now anyway."

"You think so?" I ask, feeling a bit of hope. Maybe I don't need this disguise after all. I should be able to steer clear of Guy Gisborne. Shouldn't be too hard to know when he's nearby. That foul smell of something dead is stuck in my nose.

Alan-a-Dale joins us, a large canvas bag slung over one shoulder. He's out of breath as he addresses Much. "Bad news," he announces with furrowed brows. "The sheriff's deputies have been posting Wanted posters with Robin Hood's face on it! There's a reward for his capture, dead or alive. Sounds like the sheriff doesn't like anyone else making money in *his* woods or besting his right-hand man. We have to hide Robin. Do you know where he is?"

Well, getting in trouble didn't take long. Less than a week. Must be a new record.

Alan turns to me. "Forgive me, I don't think we've met?" His expression is pleasant as he waits for an answer.

"Alan, it's me! Robin."

His eyes widen; then he throws back his head and laughs. "You don't need the Merry Men's protection. You could share a pint of ale with Guy Gisborne himself and he wouldn't recognize you. You look terrible."

"Thanks. I guess."

"But you can't wear that to the wedding tomorrow!" he exclaims. "I need handsome, charming Robin, not poor, disheveled, rotten-toothed Robin."

"But he's a wanted man," Much points out. "Elly's marrying a wealthy landowner. There could be guests there in high-up places. The sheriff himself could show up!"

Alan frowns.

"I'll still be charming on the inside," I assure him. "Plus, I wouldn't want to outshine the future groom. You got your suit?"

Alan pulls a long coat, white shirt, and black pants from his canvas bag. "Had to play from sunup to sundown, but the townsfolk were generous today. I think they felt sorry for me."

"Whatever the motivation, one look at you and Elly's going to run into your arms."

Alan appears doubtful, but squares up his shoulders and says, "Whatever happens, if not for you I'd surely be spending tomorrow curled up in a ball with my scarves over my face."

"You really love her a lot."

He thumps his chest. "She's my person."

Was it only a little over a week ago that I thought that same thing upon meeting Marian? If only she could see me now, in this disguise. She'd run for the hills! I think of her often, and hope she's feeding her brain at the school, and I admit it, I hope she thinks of me, too. Visiting her will have to wait until I'm no longer a wanted man. Whenever *that* will be.

I wake the morning of the wedding with an uneasy feeling. What was I thinking, promising to break up the wedding of two strangers? Now I'm the one who wants to curl up and hide my face.

The other Merry Men are already awake and dressed by the time I crawl out of the tent I now call home. Much helps me put my disguise back on, adding some chalk to my hair. We shovel in a breakfast of black bread and fish that sits in my stomach like a stone.

And then it's time to go. Rolo the Ratcatcher — one of the few Merry Men who has a job outside the forest — has lent us his horses and cart. Alan, Much, Little John, and I squeeze into the back next to a pile of wire cages, spring traps, and long pointy sticks stained red at the tip that we all steer clear of with a collective shudder. I wind up sticking my dagger in my belt in case we run into any trouble on the road. The Wanted poster shows me with a quiver of arrows on my back, so I leave those back at the tents. Better not to call attention.

I try not to show how nervous I am about what we're about to do, and focus on the fact that I'm being pulled along the bumpy, dusty road in a wooden cart that will no doubt collapse under our collective weight. What I wouldn't give for a working hoverboard!

By the time we arrive at the large church on the outskirts of Nottingham, the invited guests have filed in. The uninvited ones — namely, *us* — stand outside wiping dust off our clothes and hair and gathering up our nerve.

We can hear the service through the open windows. Music filters out, and I recognize Friar Tuck's voice as he starts the opening prayer. Alan-a-Dale — spiffy in his new suit — rolls his eyes. "Violin? Really? Everyone knows you need a harp at a wedding." He pulls out his small one from under his coat and puts it into position against his chest. "Ready?" he asks.

I take a deep breath and nod. "When Friar Tuck asks if anyone knows a reason they shouldn't wed, that's our signal."

We listen at the window, Alan cringing every time the groom speaks. So far we haven't heard Elly say anything at all. Finally, it's time. I pull my cap a little farther down and motion for the others to follow.

As soon as Friar Tuck says, "If anyone objects to this union, speak now, or forever hold thy peace," I throw open the doors and we march in, single file, with Alan pulling up the rear. "We object!" I announce loudly.

My voice echoes across the church, and a hundred heads in fancy headdresses and fur caps swivel around to glare at us. Religious men in friar robes stand at the end of each pew, hands clasped calmly in front of them.

"How dare you?" the groom demands, taking a step toward us. He's a burly man, gray-haired and at least twice if not three times Alan's age. But he's not as feeble as I was led to believe. He looks like he could inflict some damage with his fists, for sure.

Little John steps in front of me. The groom halts but growls at us. "What hole did *you* just crawl out of? Why have you come to ruin this sacred occasion?"

It takes me a second to remember my disguise. Maybe I laid on the ash a little too thick. Behind me Much pokes me in the back, and I shout, "Because true love is not about the number of gold coins in your pocket. Alan-a-Dale loves Elly for the goodness in her heart, and she loves him, too!"

The crowd gasps as Alan steps forward, and Elly gives a small yelp of surprise. I look at her for the first time, and I can see why Alan is smitten. Instead of the traditional wedding white, she's wearing colorful scarves draped over a plain brown dress. Kindness radiates from her as she gazes across the church at Alan.

"Is this true?" the groom asks through gritted teeth.

A tall, well-dressed man who could only be Elly's father leaps to his feet from the front row. "It doesn't matter who she loves! This union *will* happen. Now! Friar Tuck, please continue." He glares at us with such hatred that I look away. "I will deal with you later."

Friar Tuck clears his throat. "I am bound by law to only marry two people who join together willingly. If not for love, then for duty and family honor. Elly, is it your choice to marry today?"

Elly doesn't answer. She looks tearfully at her groom, then at her red-faced father, and then at Alan, who gets down on one knee. He begins to serenade her with a love song that has half the women in the room crying, and a few of the men, too. The sunlight shining through the stained-glass windows adds to the effect.

"It is indeed my choice to marry today," Elly finally says when he finishes. Alan's whole body droops. I swear I can feel his heartbreak. Then she adds, "But it is Alan-a-Dale that I want as my husband." And that's all it takes. The guests erupt in either angry shouts or happy cheers. The groom looks shocked, but to his credit he doesn't stop Elly from running into Alan's arms.

Elly's father storms down the aisle toward us, snapping his fingers at two uniformed men sitting in the back of the church by the door. The deputies from my first day! The ones who took my statues! What if they recognize me? I hunch my shoulders to try to seem smaller, as though that could help. They head toward us as well. We're trapped in the middle! I guess I should be grateful that neither the sheriff nor Guy Gisborne are here to rush us from the sides, as well!

Little John holds off Elly's father, leaving me and Much to face the deputies.

One of them has his fingertips inches from my arm

when a shout goes up on the left side of the church. Two women in huge fruit-covered hats and long black dresses start pulling at each other's hair and screaming in shrill, angry voices!

"He's mine! You stole him like a common thief!"

"I did no such thing! You need a good leeching!" Everyone — including both of the deputies — turn toward them as horrified whispers rise up though the crowd. One of the deputies begins shoving his way through the pews toward them. Now we only have one deputy to deal with.

"Look over there!" someone shouts, and points to the other side of the church. Heads then whirl around in that direction. It's one of the friars who had been standing so still beside the pews. He has jumped onto a church pew and is now waving his arms! His hood covers much of his head and face, so I can't see his expression. Has he gone crazy?

Once he has the room's attention, he bends his knees and jumps four feet straight up into the air! He lands lightly on his feet, then takes off again! The room gasps. After the second jump, the other deputy begins pushing his way toward him. Whether it's to save him from himself, or from jumping on a wedding guest, I'm not certain.

"Wow," Much says, "I didn't know anyone could jump that high! He must be part grasshopper!"

I chuckle. I've seen better. Back home, Will could do five, easy.

I know we should take advantage of the fact that at least for the moment, the focus has been taken off of us. We should get out of here and not look back. But like everyone else, I can't take my eyes off what's going on. The two young women are still shouting and pulling. One of their hats has come off now, and her braid is whipping around her head, dangerously close to slapping spectators in the face. A part of my brain registers something familiar about the color of her hair, but my attention is quickly pulled back to the jumping man.

My memory flashes back to Delta Z. Will used to practice his high jumps on the observation deck for hours, making the rest of us dizzy just watching him. He'd flap his arms to give him more lift, just like this friar is doing now. Sometimes he'd add a twist midair, and come down facing the opposite direction.

JUST LIKE THIS FRIAR IS DOING NOW.

My heart starts to pound hard in my chest. Much is pulling on my shirt, shouting in my ear that we need to get back to Rolo's cart, but I only have eyes for the flying friar, who is getting more air with each jump. His hood is inching farther back on his head with every liftoff, and I get a peek at a brown eye here, a pale cheek there.

It's not possible.

There is NO WAY it is possible.

The first deputy is only a foot away from the fighting girls, and the second one is closing in on the jumper. He spins around to avoid the deputy's reach, and his hood falls back far enough now that I can clearly see his face.

He looks right at me and shouts, "Hiya, cuz! Hang on for the ride!" Then before I can fully process what's happening, the line of friars on either side of the church rush in, lift Will (WILL!!!) off the pew by his armpits, carry him to the nearest open window, and slide him out!

I'm vaguely aware that the fighting girls are getting the same treatment. While I'm trying to process all this, two men flank me and lift me right off the ground like I weigh no more than a feather. Since both deputies have now turned their attention back to me, I see no reason to stop the friars from tossing me out a window, too.

Instead, they bring me to the front door and *then* toss me out. Will is waiting for me there, on the back of a horse! "Hop on," he says, holding on to the reins like this is something he's done every day of his life. Another horse pulls up alongside him with a pretty brown-haired girl riding in front, and a beautiful yellow-haired girl holding on to her waist. They are clearly not enemies, like their fight inside would have led everyone to believe.

"Hey, stranger," the yellow-haired girl says. *Marian.* It's Marian! "Want to hop on that horse so we can go rescue a king? Unless you're planning on staying for the wedding cake?"

"Wha . . . the king . . . huh . . . Will . . . how?" is all I can muster, I'm not proud to say.

"Not just a king," Will says, reaching out to grab my arm. "If I can get us to the sheriff's castle, can you get us past the gates?"

His horse bends at the knees, allowing me to swing my leg over its enormous flank. Is this really happening? Will (!!!) repeats his question. "Can you get us onto the grounds?"

For someone who prides himself on always knowing what to say, the power of speech continues to abandon me. The sheriff's archery tournament is today — Much and the other Merry Men have been talking about it all week. The grounds will be very crowded. It would mean seeing those awful men from the stream on our first day here, and Guy Gisborne, the deputies, and the Sheriff of Nottingham himself. But if I enter the contest, we'll get onto the grounds. Instead of trying to get all those words out, I just croak, "Yes."

"Good," Will says, trotting the horse until we're in front of the girls'. "Now hold on tight," he says, digging in his heels. "We're going to rescue King Richard."

Then he adds over his shoulder, "And your parents!"

CHAPTER TWENTY

Marian

"What did you just say?" I shout up to Will. Did he just tell Robin we're going to rescue HIS PARENTS? Is that what he couldn't tell me yesterday when we first met in town? How could Robin's parents, who are supposed to be dead, be alive on this medieval planet?

But their horse is too far ahead now, and he can't hear me over the clomping of hooves. I resign myself to having to wait for an answer until we arrive. Meanwhile, I may as well enjoy the feel of the wind in my hair and on my face. I close my eyes and trust in Kylea's control of this beast. This is a marked improvement from my behavior this morning when we first climbed on for the ride to the church. That was more of the screaming-in-terror variety.

Kylea's been great. We wouldn't have even known how to find Robin in the first place if she hadn't heard Alan-a-Dale singing about it in the village before she came to find me and Will. He'd sang about a man in green hopefully rescuing his true love from marrying another, and she put it together when she saw Will's outfit.

Kylea also came up with the idea of causing a distraction at the wedding so we could steal Robin away. She borrowed the dresses and hats from the theater department at school and had the idea to stage a fight. It turned out to be one of the most fun things I've ever done.

Friar Tuck really came through for everyone, too. We brought Will back to the school, and he explained what was going on (leaving out the part about him living on a space-port and me on another planet!). Friar Tuck said he couldn't participate in our plan (or Robin's) directly, but he wouldn't stop us, either. In the end, he agreed to provide backup in the form of his fellow friars from neighboring villages, in case they were needed. Without them, we'd likely all be in jail right now for disrupting the peace.

I'd expected the sheriff's castle to be more of, well, a *castle.* Like the way the medieval castles on Earth used to be — enormous structures with high stone walls, and moats with drawbridges, and glass towers with turrets and acres of bright green lawns. This is more like a very large house. Certainly larger than any we'd passed, but a castle? No.

It *is* surrounded by a nice lawn, at least, with a small pond in the center with a lone duck floating in it. A high fence runs around the outer perimeter, along with guards armed with arrows, swords, and quarterstaffs. An even higher fence sits closer to the house itself.

Onlookers mill about everywhere on the lawn — all sizes of men, women, and children, some taking seats on the rows of wooden stands that rise ten levels up, others shooting arrows at straw targets set up in the open fields. Banners fly in the wind and jugglers entertain the crowd. *This* was what the barman had been talking about last week! The sheriff's annual archery contest, of course! It's the perfect cover. Friar Tuck should be here soon to judge the contest. I am eager to thank him.

Will stops his horse a few yards in front of the entrance. After helping Robin off, he walks over to talk to the guard at the gate. Robin starts wobbling toward us, his legs still bowed from sitting on the horse. I hop off and hurry to meet him while Kylea ties the horses to a gatepost.

"Nice outfit," I joke. "You look awful."

He grabs my hands and swings me around. "Will said my parents are alive! And they're here!"

So I *had* heard Will right! "That's amazing! How is that possible?"

He stops swinging me but doesn't let go of my hands. I don't complain. "Apparently my parents work for the government on secret missions. King Richard had hired them years ago to search the galaxy for habitable planets where people from Earth and the other high-tech planets can go when their resources run out — which, as you know, will be soon."

Robin's parents know King Richard? The one who used to bounce me on his knee?

The words keep spilling out of him. "After years of research and traveling the galaxy, they landed on this planet. They hadn't detected it was inhabited since there's no technology here yet. They sent the disappointing report to Richard, who was about to end his own mission and return home. But the message was intercepted by Prince John. He altered it to say that Richard should come here immediately to check it out."

"So Prince John isn't hiding Richard after all?" I ask, surprised. "He actually wanted Richard to see this place so the people of Earth could move here?"

Robin shakes his head. "No, he wanted to *trap* Richard here, and my parents, too. After sending the fake letter, Prince John sent a fake reply to my parents from Richard, saying that they should remain here until he arrives. Prince John's men arrived first, and as soon as Richard's airship landed, they captured Richard and my parents. They made a deal with the local sheriff to keep them here until further notice. Must have paid him a lot of money, or promised him power. Probably both."

Out of the corner of my eye, I can see Will and Kylea at the gate, dropping arrows into a quiver that they must have talked someone into giving them. I'm not ready to give Robin up yet, so I pull him a little farther away.

"I don't understand the part you told me about getting the boxes, though, and about all of you being deleted from the interwebs?"

"I don't understand that part, either," Robin says. "Will didn't know."

I squeeze his arm. "This is huge. I'm very happy for you."

"I'm happy for you, too. If we pull this off, you'll have your king back. Then so much will change for the better for you on Earth."

He's right, I know he is. And I'm thrilled about it, of course. But I realized something the moment I saw him in the church today, when even blackened teeth and old, baggy clothes couldn't hide the glint in his bright green eyes. It wasn't only my brain that had been hungry. It was my heart, too. If we leave here, he will go one place, and I will go another, and I don't think I can bear that.

As though he knows my thoughts, he pushes my hair off my face and says, "Somehow we'll make this work."

I believe him. But all I say is, "Hey, if it doesn't, you can always go back to robbing the rich and giving to the poor."

He laughs. "How do you know about that?"

Will and Kylea return before I can tell him he's the subject of a new folk song.

"You're in," Will says, thrusting the equipment at Robin. "The first round starts in five minutes. You'll need to get through that one to get us close enough to slip into the house. Don't miss the target."

Robin rolls his eyes. "When have I ever missed the target?" He slings the quiver and bow over his shoulder and begins lacing up the armguard. "How'd you get all this stuff, anyway?"

Kylea giggles. She and Will share a look. "Best not to ask," Will says. "Just don't break any arrows or Kylea will have to marry some guy's cousin."

Robin looks over at a group of men inside the gate and groans. "Not *those* guys!"

But sure enough, it's the same group we encountered in the woods. I forgot they'd be here, too. I wish Kylea and I hadn't left our big hats at the church. "Quick, Will, give me your friar's robe. Those guys know who we are. They won't recognize Robin, but they might remember me. They'd turn him in without a second's hesitation."

Will doesn't argue; he unties the robe at the waist and slips it over his head. I slip it right back over mine and flip up the hood. We hurry past them and don't look back.

Robin takes his place in line with the other archers while the rest of us take a seat on the benches. I lean over to Will. "What's the plan for getting into the house after this?"

"Still working on that," he replies.

That doesn't inspire confidence.

A thin man dressed all in white raises a bugle to his lips and blows. He announces, "There will be five spots in the finals, and one winner. If anyone impales a spectator or another competitor with an arrow, they will be disqualified."

"Well, that's good to know," Kylea says sarcastically.

I don't see the sheriff anywhere, nor Friar Tuck, who is

supposed to be one of the judges. When I point this out to Kylea, she explains, "This is only the first round. They'll be here for the finals."

I can see why they wouldn't bring the judges out yet. The first round drags on for hours; Robin is at the end of the line. Each arrow has to be pulled out, and the area cleared again before the next archer's turn. Kylea and I are wilting. As the contestant directly before Robin steps forward and readies his bow, the man in charge announces that there is only one more spot in the finals. The first four spots have been taken by people who've gotten bull's-eyes.

The contestant lowers his bow, wipes his brow, then raises it again with steady hands. His arrow soars right into the center of the bull's-eye, and the crowd hoots and hollers. He raises his hands victoriously. The announcer shouts, "And we have our fifth!"

No one moves to get his arrow from the target like they had between the other turns. It's over!

But Robin steps forward anyway. The announcer strides toward him, waving for him to put down his bow, but Robin focuses only on the target in front of him. The crowd has quieted, everyone waiting to see what will happen.

With one swift motion, Robin loads his bow, aims, and lets his arrow fly. It slices though the air with an audible *swoosh* and splits the other man's arrow cleanly in half! The two pieces fall to the ground soundlessly, leaving Robin's arrow sticking out proudly from the center of the bull's-eye. We all jump up, shouting and cheering along with the rest of the crowd. Robin stands patiently, waiting for the announcer to reach a verdict. I hold my breath. Finally the man nods and clasps Robin on the shoulder. "We have a sixth!"

Phew! The finalists and their guests (that's us!) are led

through the taller fence, past the pond and closer to the house.

"What if I could actually win this?" Robin says, his eyes bright. "I could give the money to the Merry Men."

Will tilts his head at him. "You? Giving money away?"

He shrugs. "Maybe I've changed."

"Sorry," Will says. "As noble as it is, we can't dangle you right beneath the sheriff's nose. It's too risky. This is our chance to get in the house."

Kylea suddenly gasps. "I don't think you'll need to." She points at the side of the house, where five people have just emerged. A mustached man dressed all in black with a silver star on his chest is first. This can only be the infamous Sheriff of Nottingham. He's followed closely by the two deputies from the wedding. They're leading out a man and woman who blink hard against the sunlight as though they haven't seen it in a while. A tall, broad-shouldered man with a beard and a grim expression steps into view last.

My heart thumps. I've never seen him with a beard before. Men in The City are all clean-shaven. But it's him. It's King Richard! Kylea stretches out her arm to bar me from running to him. I hadn't even realized my feet had started to move!

The deputies push them into chairs beside a raised wooden platform. They all three tilt their faces up to the sun, eyes closed. The woman wraps her arms around herself, almost protectively.

"It's them," Robin says, his voice shaking. "Those are my parents."

And of course they have to be. Robin looks exactly like a younger version of his father. And he has his mother's way of walking that almost makes it look like they're skimming the ground.

Will's arm shoots out to block Robin, who, like me, had started to move forward. "Wait," Will says firmly. "We'll have our chance, but it's not now."

Robin looks like he's about to argue, but then nods and steps back.

"I had sort of expected them to be trapped in a dungeon or hidden in a high tower," I admit to the others, "like in the old stories. But they're not even handcuffed or anything. Not that I wish they were, of course."

Will nods. "Your grandmother's sources told her that Prince John paid the sheriff handsomely to keep them here, but instructed him not to treat them too harshly. He must have felt being trapped on this planet was punishment enough. They can't leave without a ship, and he took theirs away."

"Speaking of ships," Robin asks him, "where's yours?"

Will points to the woods beyond the house. "Due east. The coordinates led me right here."

Once the new target has been set in place, the sheriff climbs up onto the raised platform and opens his arms wide. He smiles, but it doesn't look friendly. It looks annoyed. And bored. Not a good combination. "Will the five — I mean six — remaining contestants please step forward."

Will looks pained, with his lips tight and his brows furrowed. "You'll have to see it through," he tells Robin. "The sheriff doesn't know who you are. Let's keep it that way."

"Got it, boss," Robin says, tightening his armguard again. "I'll try not to rupture anyone's spleen with my arrows. Even the sheriff's."

Will starts to laugh, and then hiccups. That makes me and Kylea laugh, even though I don't know why rupturing a spleen is funny.

Robin takes his place next to the others. He's the youngest by a decade, but in his disguise no one could tell. One of the bald brothers who had bragged of his prowess with the bow and arrow is also among the finalists.

"Step forward and announce yourself," the sheriff calls out. I look around for Friar Tuck but still don't see him. Perhaps he got held up at the wedding.

One by one the men step forward and give their names. The crowd cheers and boos in equal measure. Robin is fifth in line, staring right at his parents, who are seated only ten yards away from us. What is he waiting for? Surely he won't give his real name. Not when he's on Wanted posters? After what feels like an eternity, Robin says, "My name is . . . Will Stutely."

I let the air out. Beside me, I hear Will exhale with relief as well. Then, as the last man steps forward and opens his mouth, Robin speaks again. "No, that is a lie. My name is Robin. Robin of Locksley. And you have kidnapped my parents." Then, as an afterthought, he adds, "And a king. I have come to take them back."

A hush falls across the crowd. Will, Kylea, and I sink down in our seats.

Should have seen *that* coming.

CHAPTER TWENTY-ONE

⤙ Robin ⤚

At first the sheriff doesn't move. He squints at me, as though trying to connect my name with the image of the person in the poster. "It is the man who ruined the wedding!" one of the deputies cries, shading his eyes to see me better.

Slowly, menacingly, the sheriff turns toward my parents. "Do you claim this man as your son, this outlaw who dresses in rags to lie and cheat his way into MY home?"

Before my parents can reply, King Richard jumps up from his seat and comes bounding toward me. The crowd gasps, and one of the deputies hurries after him. He has a dagger in his belt but has not reached for it. Perhaps he's hoping the king will attack me for him.

But the king walks right by me and straight to Marian. She rises to her feet, her back straight and head high. She curtsies. "Hello, Your Majesty."

"Marian Fitzwalter?" he asks, his eyes wide.

"Yes, Your Majesty."

He sweeps her into his arms. "Marian! Little Marian all grown up into a beautiful young lady! I would know that lovely voice anywhere! You are a sight for sore eyes!"

Marian laughs, and I can hear the relief in it. "It is good to see you, too. I wasn't sure if you'd remember me."

"Of course!" he booms. "You were the only child who

laughed at my jokes!" He stands back to look at her. "But how are you here?"

Marian looks at me, and then back at the king. "It is a long story. But it must wait." She gestures to me.

"Oh yes, of course," the king says. "Family comes first."

"They are not family!" the sheriff shouts from the platform. He whips around to face my parents. "Tell him he is mistaken and he is holding up the contest!" he bellows.

My father rises, resting his hand on my mom's shoulder. She places a hand over his. "Our son," my father begins. Then his voice cracks. "Our son . . . well, he wouldn't look anything like you. I'm sorry."

My heart sinks. Does my father so fear the sheriff's wrath that he would respond this way? Will comes to stand beside me, and I'm grateful for the support. "Your disguise," he whispers.

Of course! I snatch off the wool hat, which has matted down my hair with sweat, and look back up.

They still look at me blankly, this time with pity in their eyes. I look around at the crowd. Half have that same pitying look, the other half look angry. They want to get on with the contest, I'm sure. I can tell by the way the sheriff is clenching his fists that he's close to exploding. I have to do something. There's only one option left.

"Maybe this will help," I say, dashing a few feet away to the pond. I stick my head under the water, scrubbing at my face as I do it. I emerge, flipping my head back so my hair flies off my face. Then I pull off the clothes to reveal my old green outfit from home. I'd worn it to give me confidence at the church. For a final touch, I yank my hat out of my pocket and plop it on my head. Then I smooth out the feather. Hopefully my father will recognize it.

Their reaction is instant. Growing up, I never imagined what it would be like to meet my parents, so I'm completely unprepared for the scene that is playing out now. My mother flies from the wooden platform — I swear her feet don't even touch the ground. Then her hands are on my face, in my hair, her tears are flowing, and she's making sounds that I'm not sure are supposed to come from a human. Like a cross between a squeak and a moan.

My father is here now, too. "You look just like me," he says, his voice both foreign and familiar at the same time.

My mother is holding me now and rocking back and forth. "You've had a good life, right?" she keeps saying. "You're happy and healthy?"

I nod my head, but I'm not sure she can tell. "Uncle Kent took very good care of me. Delta Z was great, and Will here —"

"We were going to explain it all when you got a little older," she insists, too worked up to even glance over at Will. "We couldn't take you where we had to go. We'd committed to this life of service, but it's a dangerous one. We wanted you to have a stable life, and then when you were old enough to decide for yourself, we'd welcome you with open arms if you wanted to join us." She burst into a new round of tears. "We thought it was best if we just left you once rather than leaving you over and over again. I hope we didn't make a mistake."

"I thought you were dead," I manage to squeeze out. "All your boxes . . . they got delivered to Delta Z. And then we all got erased . . . records of us, I mean."

My mother makes that strangling sound again. "I'm so sorry. Prince John must have sent our belongings when he took our ship. In case anything happened to us, we'd left instructions for you to receive them when you were older.

He must have wanted to make sure no one would come searching for us. And most important to him, no one would know about the important work we were doing."

The sheriff's deputy suddenly yanks her away. I'm too stunned to react in time. My father does, though.

"Hey!" he shouts, pulling her back. King Richard storms toward the deputy, fury on his face. The sheriff bellows, "Enough! Everyone, stand down!"

Something in the tone of his voice shocks everyone into letting go of one another. During our reunion, ten more of the sheriff's men have come to stand in a circle around us, effectively trapping us all in the center. I still have my dagger, but my bow and arrow are behind me, out of reach. My parents and the king are not armed. Marian, Will, and Kylea huddle close together. King Richard spreads his arms out in front of all of us, like a human shield. My father moves into the same position on the other side. He winks at me, and his eyes sparkle with defiance. Marian shakes her head. "No doubt about it, he's your dad."

"No, *you* stand down," another voice calls out from behind us, a calmer voice, but commanding nonetheless.

"Friar Tuck!" Marian shouts in surprise. We all twist around to see him approaching through the crowd.

And he's not alone. All the friars from the church this morning are with him. And so are Little John and Much and the rest of the Merry Men from the forest! They've risked capture for me! My hand tightens on my dagger. I'm not going to let harm come to any of them. Little John starts to storm over as soon as he sees us trapped in the circle, but Friar Tuck holds him back.

The sheriff's men and the friars all have swords at the ready now, pointing at one another. I'd put the odds in our favor, but only slightly. And then the sheriff whistles. Twenty men on horseback ride onto the field from behind the house. I flinch when I see Guy Gisborne in the lead. They pull up in front of the platform, load their bows, and await orders.

Our odds have just gone down. Considerably.

"Let us leave," King Richard calls out, his voice rich and deep and kingly. "We have no quarrel with you, nor you with us. Keep my brother's payment, or split it among the poor farmers you have been unfairly taxing for years."

The crowd leaps to their feet. In response, the line of guards on horseback raise their bows. The crowd leans back, like they're one person instead of a hundred.

The sheriff shouts, "Who are you to tell me how to run my town?" He makes a tiny gesture with his finger, and the battle begins! Arrows fly, shields are raised, and swords are drawn! My father immediately grabs the girls and my mother, taking them behind the stands where at least there is a little shelter.

"I want to help!" I hear Marian call out.

"Help by staying safe," my father replies.

And then I'm swept up in it. Some of the spectators have risen to fight as well. Perhaps they've just been waiting for the right opportunity, and we've given it to them. I lose sight of the sheriff as three of his men protect him, swords swinging at anyone who comes near.

Rolo the Ratcatcher runs toward me with his spear, clearing a path through the first circle as the deputies scatter to get out of his way. Much tosses me my sword, and I hand him my dagger. He points it at one guard, then another, to keep them at bay while I come out swinging. I clash swords with any of the sheriff's men who come my way.

Practicing with Little John this week has made me practically unbeatable. Anyone unarmed I let pass.

Little John and Guy Gisborne are facing off near the pond with quarterstaffs. They seem evenly matched. By their moves, I'd guess this isn't their first time dueling together, and I doubt it will be their last.

Arrows fly over my head toward the line of men on horseback, and I turn to find their origin. I'm not surprised to see Marian has taken up my bow. Her last arrow whizzes through one guard's hair, knocking him right off his horse! She only has time to yelp in victory before my father yanks her away again.

One of the deputies from the wedding has caught up with me. He swings his sword at my leg before I can fully turn away. It hits broadside. The pain goes up my leg, and while I'm slowed by it, he slices at my arm. I push aside the pain and turn on him. We clash swords until I feel like my arm is going to fall off. It's impossible to tell by the number of men limping or bleeding or both which side, if any, is winning.

"ENOUGH!" The sheriff's voice rises above the yells and clangs of metal on metal. I'm surprised to see King Richard is standing close to his side. The fighting grinds to a halt, but not before I snatch the pouch dangling from my opponent's belt. "Just taking back what's mine," I tell him.

"This day is not about fighting," the sheriff shouts. "It is about getting together in the name of friendly competition. I call a cease-fire." His men immediately drop their weapons to their sides. The rest of us pause to make sure it's not a trick, then we do the same. King Richard gives an almost imperceptible nod of approval.

Marian rushes out to stand beside me. Kylea and my parents follow. "That's what he does," she says admiringly. "King Richard brokers peace, even out here."

My father and I share a nod of understanding. I decide not to point out to Marian that Richard currently has the tip of a dagger sticking into the sheriff's back.

I step toward the men. "My parents are coming home with me."

The sheriff shakes his head. Gotta hand it to him, he's holding his ground even with a dagger at his back.

The crowd growls in dissent again, but King Richard holds up his hand for silence.

Will suddenly steps out in front of us, a large purple bruise growing on his cheek. "Maybe this will help convince you," he says calmly. Then he turns toward the pond and lifts up his hand. He points one finger at the lone duck, swimming in a lazy circle.

"Poof," he says.

And all the water in the pond disappears.

A hundred shocked gasps rise into the air. The duck falls to the ground in surprise, then shakes her tail feathers and waddles onto the lawn.

Marian runs over to Will. "You have a vapor gun! Those were still in development when I left Earth. It's supposed to turn gases into water for people to drink. I guess it works in reverse, too! How did you get it?"

"Your grandmother sent it up with the ship," he says, sliding something into his pocket. "Cool, right?"

"I'm going to have a long talk with good ol' Grandma when I get home," Marian says, shaking her head. "She's chock-full of surprises."

The sheriff finally pulls his eyes away from the pond-shaped hole left on his front lawn. "Fine, take them!" he says, all the fight gone from his voice. "They were eating me out of house and home anyway. Now get off my property immediately." He pushes past King Richard and storms into his house.

"Here," Will says, quickly pulling a small device out of his back pocket. He hands it to me. I look up in surprise.

"You brought a medi-gun!"

He nods. "There was a first aid kit in the ship. You're bleeding pretty bad."

I rest it in my hand, fully aware now of the throbbing in my leg and the line of blood running down past my elbow.

Friar Tuck hurries over to us. "The sheriff won't stay quiet for long. You should go."

"Take this," I tell him, pressing the medi-gun into his hand. "Pull this trigger here, and one injection will allow the injured to recover quickly. Offer to both sides, if you like. There should be enough in there for everyone."

"I will," he promises. "And you will take our horses where you need to go. They know how to find their way back to us."

"Thank you," I say. "For everything. Oh, I have one more thing for you." I pick up the deputy's pouch laying at my feet and pull out the little golden statue. "This reminds me of you. You can sell it and use the money for the school."

My mother watches this exchange, then laughs. "I remember that statue! I made it in high school out of that leftover gold resin from the lab. Kent modeled for the class."

"I remember that," my father says, laughing, too. "Kent complained it was cold clad only in his underwear! You really captured his likeness."

"What?" Will and I exclaim at the same time. The statue doesn't look anything like Uncle Kent!

"He ate more than his share of vita-squares then," my father explains.

"And he was *bald*?" Will asks. "Dad is very proud of his hair."

My mother shakes her head. "He wasn't bald. I just couldn't figure out how to make hair!"

"I'll take it," Friar Tuck says, sticking the statue in his robe before I can change my mind about giving it away. He leaves to help prepare the horses, and my father pulls me aside.

"We were able to watch the first round of the contest from the window," he tells me. "It's been our only view since we got here. I was rooting for you to win even before I knew who you were. Where'd you learn to shoot like that?"

I grin. "Virtual reality archery game. I'll teach you when we get home."

"Deal," he says.

I reach up and pull off my hat. "You should have this. You wore one just like it in a picture from before you were captured. We had to make them in class. The feather was stuck in with your boxes."

He takes the hat and runs his fingers over the feather. "You made this back on Delta Z?"

"Actually, Will made it and I stole it. Mine came out the worst in the class. I'm not very crafty."

"I think you've proved yourself plenty crafty," he says, placing the hat back on my head. "It looks better on you."

I grin. "True! I *am* the more handsome of the two of us."

Dad laughs and slaps me playfully on the back. "Oh, this is going to be fun!"

CHAPTER TWENTY-TWO

Marian

King Richard has gone ahead to the ship so he can send communications to the resistance to let them know he's coming home. I'm about to head over to say goodbye to Friar Tuck when Robin pulls me aside. "Is it okay with you if I let Little John and Much know where to find the wreckage of the *Solar Hammer*? They could scavenge whatever they can use from it and sell off the rest. It would be enough to get them food and better shelter, maybe even enough to pay off their debts to the sheriff."

"Of course," I tell him. "That's a great idea."

He squeezes my arm in thanks and runs off to tell them. He's definitely changed, all right.

Now that I'm faced with my final goodbyes, a lump has formed in my throat. Friar Tuck sees me approaching the horses and comes over to me.

I gather my nerve and say, "You knew when we met that I hadn't come to Sherwood Forest to be your new student, right?"

He smiles gently, but only says, "You are definitely meant to be a student, Marian. Whether you study with me or not, there's a hunger for knowledge in you, and you will do great things with it."

I wish I could take Friar Tuck home with me!

He reaches into his robe and pulls out my grandmother's headpiece. "I was never going to keep this."

I reach for it, then pull back. "I'd like you to have it. That way you'll always remember me."

"Are you certain?" he asks.

I nod. The crown doesn't mean the same thing to me now that I know what it really is. I've tasted freedom now. I won't be tracked again. "I'll make a deal with you. I'll trade it for one orange. Wait, two oranges."

"Done," he says, and plucks them from yet another robe pocket.

I burst out laughing. "You just happen to carry two oranges with you?"

He pulls out a third. "Learning to juggle."

I reach over and give Friar Tuck a hug. His robe isn't as scratchy as I thought it would be. Kylea comes up and puts her arm through mine. "My turn," she says. I slip the oranges in my dress pocket, give the friar one last pat on the arm, and let Kylea pull me away.

"Here," she says, pulling off her beaded bracelet. The colors are glowing bright in the late afternoon sun. "We never had a chance to make yours in crafts class. I want you to have mine. When you need to remember to breathe, close your eyes and let your fingers count each bead, one by one, as they slide over them. You can repeat a word to yourself as you do it. I suggest *Kylea*. Ky . . . le . . . a. That has a nice, calming ring to it, right?"

I throw my arms around her. "It's the most beautiful thing I've ever owned." And I mean it. "I'll never forget your spirit and everything you've done for me." I motion to the group, now waiting impatiently for us to finish. Well, Will is waiting impatiently. He's anxious to figure out how to fit all of us in the transport ship. The rest are too busy catching up to worry about it. "Everything you've done for *us*," I finish.

She waves it off. "It was nothing."

"There's a necklace in my suitcase in our room," I tell her. "It's yours now."

"The gold one with the pearl that glides along it?" she asks.

My eyes widen, and then I laugh. "You snoop!"

She shrugs. "I had to find out *something* about my new roommate. Never suspected she came from the stars."

We laugh together and then cry together. Then Will comes over and drags me away. The horses are lined up and ready to go. Robin puts out his hand to help me up on my horse, but I don't take it. I've gotten stronger. I can easily do it myself. "You clean up good," I tell him as I slide into the saddle. "Green's your color."

"Every color pales in comparison to you," Robin replies from atop his own horse. From anyone else his words would have sounded corny.

Will leans over and slaps Robin on the back. "Nice, cuz! You've finally got game!"

Robin winces. Will's hand must have touched a sore spot. I noticed neither he nor Will used the medi-gun on themselves.

He recovers quickly and says, "Yeah, well, I learned from the best. Thanks for coming halfway across the galaxy to find me, by the way."

"Anytime," Will says, picking up his reins. "Race you back to the ship?"

Robin shakes his head. Then he winks at me, digs in his heels, and takes off, due east. "Hey!" Will shouts, then gallops after him. Robin's father calls out "Eat my dust!" and off he goes.

Robin's mother pulls up alongside me and shakes her head. "Boys." Then she turns to look at me. "So, it's not every day a mother gets to meet her son and her future daughter-in-law on the same afternoon."

I'm so startled by her comment that I don't know what to say. She winks, shouts "To the ship!" and takes off.

I sigh. Looks like I'll have my hands full keeping up with this family. I feel to make sure my new bracelet is in place and take a deep breath before directing my horse into the woods. They may be in a rush to get to the ship, but I'm not. I plan to savor every tree and flower and bird that I pass.

When I finally arrive at the ship, Robin greets me with a goofy grin. "We have company," he says.

"Uh-oh, that's never good."

"This time it is," he promises. I climb into the ship after him. It's bigger than the *Solar Hammer*, but not by much. Extra straps have been secured in place along the sides, with makeshift seats for all the extra passengers.

And curled up in the driver's seat is none other than Deedee.

Will hurries in, shaking his head. "Don't even think about it," he warns us. "It's too crowded as it is."

Deedee lazily opens one eye, sticks out her tongue, and licks Will's hand. Then she goes back to dozing.

Will sighs. "Fine. But *you're* going to have to explain him to the commander!"

"Her," I correct him.

"Mind if I drive?" King Richard asks Will, who jumps out of the way. "Of course not, Your Majesty." But King

Richard still can't sit down due to a deer being in the way. When Will slides into the copilot's seat, Deedee gets up, stretches, and climbs onto his lap before closing her eyes again.

"Looks like Princess Nosey Spots likes him better than you now," I whisper to Robin, clicking my chest harness into place.

"I thought *I* was Princess Nosey Spots," he whispers back as he checks my straps and then clicks his own into place.

I shake my head. "Nope. You're Robin Hood. Little kids sing folktales about you."

"They do?"

"Don't go getting a big head about it, now."

"Who, me?"

I reach for his hand and we zoom off into the stars.

About the Author

Wendy Mass is the *New York Times* bestselling author of twenty-four novels for young readers, including *The Candymakers*, *Bob* (co-written by Rebecca Stead), and the Twice Upon a Time, Willow Falls, and Space Taxi series. She is helping her family build a labyrinth in their backyard while working on her next book. Not at the same time, of course. That'd be weird. Visit her at wendymass.com.